Collins

SNAP REVISION

LORD OF THE FLIES

AQA GCSE English Literature

CHARLOTTE WOOLLEY

REVISE SET TEXTS IN A SNAP

Published by Collins
An imprint of HarperCollinsPublishers
1 London Bridge Street,
London, SE1 9GF

9780008247164

First published 2017

10 9 8 7 6 5 4 3 2

British Library Cataloguing in Publication Data.

A CIP record of this book is available from the
British Library.

Printed in the Italy by Grafica Veneta S.p.A.

Commissioning Editor: Gillian Bowman
Managing Editor: Craig Balfour
Author: Charlotte Wooley
Copyeditor: David Christie
Proofreaders: Jill Laidlaw and Louise Robb
Project management and typesetting:
  Mark Steward
Cover designers: Kneath Associates and
  Sarah Duxbury
Production: Natalia Rebow

ACKNOWLEDGEMENTS

Quotations from *Lord of the Flies* by William
Golding © *Lord of the Flies*, William Golding,
Faber and Faber Ltd.

The author and publisher are grateful to the
copyright holders for permission to use quoted
materials and images.

Every effort has been made to trace copyright
holders and obtain their permission for the use of
copyright material. The author and publisher will
gladly receive information enabling them to rectify
any error or omission in subsequent editions. All
facts are correct at time of going to press.

Contents

Plot

Chapters 1 and 2   4
Chapters 3 and 4   6
Chapters 5 and 6   8
Chapters 7 and 8   10
Chapters 9 and 10   12
Chapters 11 and 12   14
Narrative Structure   16

Setting and Context

The Island   18
Golding's Background   20
Historical – The Impact of War   22
Literary Adventures and
  Boys' Fiction   24

Characters

Ralph   26
Jack   28
Piggy   30
Simon   32
Roger   34
The Beast   36
Sam and Eric   38
The Littluns   40

Themes

Power and Leadership   42
Civilisation and Society   44
Death and Violence   46
Fear   48
Religion   50
Innocence   52
Identity   54
Friendship   56

The Exam

Tips and Assessment Objectives   58
Practice Questions   60
Planning a Character Question
  Response   62
Grade 5 Annotated Response   64
Grade 7+ Annotated Response   66
Planning a Theme Question
  Response   68
Grade 5 Annotated Response   70
Grade 7+ Annotated Response   72

Glossary   74
Answers   76

You must be able to: explore how Golding introduces his characters and themes in the first two chapters.

The setting

The island on which the boys crash is a typical paradise, with a beach, blue sky and tropical lagoons. But underneath this beauty is the dangerous side of nature – **oppressive** heat, fallen trees and dark forest.

What are the characters' relationships?

Ralph and Piggy meet first. Ralph is dismissive but not unkind, although Piggy is fat, ugly and suffers from asthma. He's also from a different class to Ralph, suggested by his accent and orphaned status. But Piggy is quickly established as the most intelligent boy, recognising the conch in the water and knowing how to use it as a summons.

Jack leads the choir, and assumes he should lead all the boys, but they vote for Ralph. Ralph, Jack and Simon explore the island but find it uninhabited. They're excited by adventure, and make their mark including pushing a large rock down the mountainside, **foreshadowing** Piggy's death later.

Jack tries to kill a pig but fails, and is embarrassed in front of the others: 'He snatched his knife out of the sheath and slammed it into a tree trunk. Next time there would be no mercy'.

How are ideas of fear and destruction introduced?

At the next meeting, a small boy with a birthmark tells them he's seen a 'beastie'. Ralph dismisses it as nightmares or their fear making them see monsters in the unfamiliar world around them. But Jack tells the boy he'll hunt for it and the littluns are still afraid that it might be real.

Ralph decides they need a fire that creates smoke to attract the attention of passing ships that might rescue them. The boys don't stop to think, just run up the mountain in excitement and snatch Piggy's glasses to start a fire. The fire gets out of control. By the time it burns itself out, part of the island has been destroyed. They realise the boy with the birthmark is missing – the first death on the island.

Key Quotations to Learn

[The ground was] torn everywhere by the upheavals of fallen trees ... always, almost visible, was the heat. (Chapter 1)

[Ralph] danced out into the hot air of the beach and then returned as a fighter-plane, with wings swept back, and machine-gunned Piggy. (Chapter 1)

What intelligence had been shown was traceable to Piggy while the most obvious leader was Jack. But there was a stillness about Ralph as he sat that marked him out. (Chapter 1)

'We want to have fun. And we want to be rescued.' (Ralph: Chapter 2)

Summary

- The boys have crashed on the island, without any surviving grown-ups.
- They elect Ralph as a leader but Jack takes responsibility for the hunters.
- The boys decide to use the conch to control who speaks when.
- They start a fire on the mountain to provide smoke for rescue but it burns out of control, possibly killing a littlun.

Questions

QUICK TEST
1. Who are the main four characters in the novel?
2. How did the boys get to the island?
3. What are the littluns afraid of?
4. How does the **conflict** between Jack and Piggy begin?
5. What is the immediate result of the fire on the mountain?

EXAM PRACTICE
Using one of the 'Key Quotations to Learn', write a paragraph analysing the way that Golding introduces the themes of the novel.

You must be able to: explore how Golding presents the increasing conflict between the boys.

How does Jack change in these chapters?

Jack becomes more **savage** and **animalistic**, as he becomes obsessed with hunting. He paints his face with mud, trying to create camouflage but ends up not recognising himself. Jack also neglects his responsibilities and lets the fire go out because of his obsession with hunting. When confronted by Ralph, he responds violently, punching Piggy and breaking his glasses.

What happens to the littluns?

Mostly, they carry on day-to-day and don't think too much about home, except in their nightmares. But they do suffer constant illness because of poor diet. When Henry, Percival and Johnny are playing, Roger throws stones at them but, at the moment, the memory of adult disapproval is enough to make him avoid hitting them.

How do the boys begin to divide?

The hunters begin to separate from the other boys, following Jack as he promises them games of hunting and feasting, while Ralph and Simon work on building shelters. Although this protects the whole group, the littluns are mostly neglected by the older boys. Simon is the only one who takes the time to look after them, finding them fruit to eat when he goes into the forest. Simon seeks **solitude** away from both groups, alone in the forest amid the peace of nature.

What happens with the fire?

Ralph, Piggy and Simon see a ship out at sea, but realise that the fire has gone out. It was the responsibility of Jack and his hunters to keep the fire burning, and Jack doesn't seem to understand the severity of what has happened – that they could have been rescued but they failed to attract the ship's attention.

Key Quotations to Learn

'But you like it!' shouted Ralph. 'You want to hunt! While I—' ... He wanted to explain how people were never quite what you thought they were. (Chapter 3)

The candle-buds opened their wide white flowers glimmering under the light that pricked down from the first stars. (Chapter 3)

Jack, faced at once with too many awful implications, ducked away from them. (Chapter 4)

Jack was powerless and raged without knowing why. By the time the pile was built, they were on different sides of a high barrier. (Chapter 4)

[Ralph] turned away and walked off, down the mountain. (Chapter 4)

Summary

- Jack becomes more obsessed with hunting, and more savage in his behaviour.
- Simon values privacy and dislikes conflict, but helps the littluns when they often get ignored.
- Roger throws stones at a littlun but doesn't hit him.
- A ship passes by because the hunters have let the fire go out.

Questions

QUICK TEST
1. How do Ralph and Simon look after the boys?
2. What relationship does Simon have with the littluns?
3. What is Roger's reaction to the littluns?
4. What effect is the island having on Jack?
5. What happens with the signal fire?

EXAM PRACTICE
Using one of the 'Key Quotations to Learn', write a paragraph analysing the way that Golding increases the conflict between Jack and Ralph.

Chapters 5 and 6

You must be able to: explore how ideas about the Beast, and the characters of the boys, develop in these chapters.

How does Ralph change through these chapters?

Ralph calls an assembly to tell the rest of the boys that they need to do what he instructs them. He reminds them that the fire is the most important thing to get them rescued. He is frustrated by their failure to realise the danger they're in, as they keep treating their situation as a game.

Jack leads the hunters away. Ralph knows he can't risk blowing the conch because if they don't come back he will lose his authority and **credibility**.

When Sam and Eric describe their encounter with the 'beast', Ralph leads a search to find it and bravely volunteers to go first. He is again frustrated by the boys' lack of understanding of their situation.

How do the littluns show their fear?

The littluns listen seriously to Ralph, seeing him as a grown-up in charge. One tells the assembly about having a nightmare and waking up to see something 'horrid' moving in the forest.

Percival Wemyss Madison repeats his name and address to Ralph, as he's been taught to do at home when he gets lost so that he can be safely found.

What do we learn about the Beast?

The older boys have different attitudes to the Beast. Ralph and Piggy comfort the boys and tell them it's imaginary – just a nightmare. Then they explain logically that there can't be a monster on an island this small.

Jack argues that he's a hunter and has explored the island on his own and not seen a beast.

Simon, though, expresses further doubt. He tries to explain that he thinks the Beast isn't a monstrous animal, but something inside them to be afraid of; however, he can't make himself understood and the rest of the boys tell Ralph they think it is a monster.

A dead parachutist, killed in an aerial battle above the island, falls to the ground. His parachute gets tangled in the trees so that every time the wind blows he seems to move. Eric and Sam, tending the fire, see him and mistake him for the Beast, prompting a search across the island.

Key Quotations to Learn

To Ralph, seated, this seemed the breaking up of sanity. Fear, beasts, no general agreement that the fire was all-important. (Chapter 5)

Simon became inarticulate in his effort to express mankind's essential illness. (Chapter 5)

Soon the darkness was full of claws, full of the awful unknown and menace. (Chapter 6)

'What a place for a fort!' (Jack: Chapter 6)

'I'm chief. I'll go. Don't argue.' (Ralph: Chapter 6)

Summary

- Ralph calls an assembly to lay down rules that the boys need to follow, exerting his authority.
- They discuss the Beast, and Simon suggests it's something in them.
- The rest of the boys are afraid it's something ghost-like or monstrous.
- A dead parachutist lands on the island and gets tangled in the trees.

Questions

QUICK TEST
1. Why does Ralph call an assembly?
2. What do the boys at the assembly say about the Beast?
3. Who is the parachutist?
4. What role do Sam and Eric play in these chapters?
5. What happens on the search of the island?

EXAM PRACTICE
Using one of the 'Key Quotations to Learn', write a paragraph analysing the response of the boys to the idea of the Beast.

Chapters 7 and 8

You must be able to: explain how the boys become more savage in these chapters.

How do the boys become more savage?

The boys tried, but failed at first, to kill a pig. In a **ritualistic** re-enactment, they re-play the hunt with Robert acting as the pig. During this, the boys are described as chanting, almost **frenzied**, foreshadowing Simon's death in Chapter 9.

After the boys divide into two groups, the hunters successfully kill a pig. In celebration, the boys mount its head on a stick and dab their faces with its blood. Jack also calls it a 'gift' to the beast, which has tribal **undertones** of sacrifice and worship, suggesting that they are going back to a pre-Christian religion.

How does the conflict between Jack and Ralph develop further?

Recalling the pig-hunt, Ralph and Jack compete for the boys' attention and respect. They search together for the beast, finding the parachutist and mistaking his body for a monster. Each boy tries to be braver than the other.

Jack, frustrated with Ralph's popularity and success, as well as his friendship with Piggy, calls a vote to see if the boys think he should be leader instead. When nobody votes for him he's humiliated, and leaves the group to form a new hunting tribe.

What is Simon's experience in the forest?

Simon goes alone into the forest and finds the pig's head rotting on a stick. The heat, the sight of it and his illness (which has caused him to faint before) combine to leave him hallucinating that the pig's head speaks to him. Golding calls it 'the Lord of the Flies', a name from the Bible for the devil. He hears the head/devil telling him that the evil is in the boys themselves and that Simon needs to let it 'have fun'.

Key Quotations to Learn

... clothes, worn away, stiff like his own with sweat, put on, not for **decorum** or comfort but out of custom: the skin of the body, scurfy with brine ... He [Ralph] discovered with a little fall of the heart that these were the conditions he took as normal now and that he did not mind. (Chapter 7)

The creature lifted its head, holding toward them the ruin of a face. (Chapter 7)

'You'll get back to where you came from.' (Simon: Chapter 7)

'Kill the pig! Cut his throat! Kill the pig! Bash him in!' (All the boys, chanting: Chapter 7)

'You want a real pig,' said Robert, still caressing his rump, 'because you've got to kill him.' 'Use a littlun,' said Jack, and everybody laughed. (Chapter 7)

'I'm not going to play any longer. Not with you.' (Jack: Chapter 8)

Summary

- Ralph dreams of home, missing food and a hot bath – symbolic of society and its loss.
- The boys carry out a successful hunt. They put the pig's head on a stick as a sacrifice.
- They re-enact the hunt in tribal celebration.
- Simon, alone in the forest, sees the pig's head and has a fit, hallucinating that it speaks to him.

Questions

QUICK TEST
1. What effect does the hunt have on Ralph and Jack?
2. What do the boys do after the hunt?
3. Why does Jack leave the group?
4. What is the Lord of the Flies?
5. How is it possible for the dead head to speak to Simon?

EXAM PRACTICE
Using one of the 'Key Quotations to Learn', write a paragraph analysing the way the conflict between the boys increases.

Chapters 9 and 10

You must be able to: understand Simon's death and its aftermath.

What happens to Simon?

After recovering from his fit, Simon starts to leave and tells the boys that they are the evil on the island. He finds the parachutist and stops long enough to realise that the body is not a monster or beast.

He stumbles into the middle of the boys' frenzied tribal dance in the thunderstorm and, in the heat of the moment, they don't recognise him. Simon is beaten to death while trying to warn them. As the rain stops, the boys stop too and drift away.

Simon's body is covered by bright creatures, like lights or candles, and his body is washed out to sea.

What are the different responses of the boys?

Ralph doesn't shy away from responsibility although he has difficulty talking about it. He insists that they call it murder, but tells Piggy 'you were outside the circle', suggesting he sees Piggy as more innocent.

Piggy tries to find ways to suggest that maybe Simon was alive after all or that it wasn't their fault, blaming the storm, their fear and Simon himself for wandering in the way he did. He is ashamed when Ralph says 'Oh, Piggy', in a 'low and stricken voice', but tells Ralph not to discuss it with Sam and Eric. Neither Sam or Eric admit their part, but tell the others they, too, left early.

Jack doesn't acknowledge Simon's death, except as an intrusion of 'the beast' into their feast. He concludes that the beast disguised itself and, in any case, can't be killed.

What happens when Jack's tribe comes to the beach?

They come in darkness to steal Piggy's glasses and arrive unexpectedly. During the fight, Ralph and Eric end up unknowingly fighting each other, a **metaphor** for the chaos and internal conflict of the boys. Jack successfully steals the glasses, but leaves the conch, not understanding its importance.

Key Quotations to Learn

There was the throb and stamp of a single **organism**. (Chapter 9)

The crowd surged after it, poured down the rock, leapt on to the beast, screamed, struck, bit, tore. (Chapter 9)

The water rose farther and dressed Simon's coarse hair with brightness. The line of his cheek silvered and the turn of his shoulder became sculptured marble. (Chapter 9)

'You were outside. Outside the circle. You never really came in. Didn't you see what we – what they did?' (Ralph: Chapter 10)

He [Jack] was a chief now in truth; and he made stabbing motions with his spear. From his left hand dangled Piggy's broken glasses. (Chapter 10)

Summary

- Simon, leaving the head behind, stumbles across the parachutist and sees it for what it really is.
- Ralph and Piggy join the rest of the hunters at a feast during a thunderstorm, which turns into a tribal dance.
- Simon comes into the chaos, and is murdered by the other boys.
- The next day, Ralph and Piggy try to talk about what they have done.
- Jack's tribe feel no remorse over Simon's death. They come and steal Piggy's glasses.

Questions

QUICK TEST
1. What does Simon do at the opening of the chapter?
2. What drives the boys to kill Simon?
3. What happens to Simon's body?
4. How do Ralph, Piggy, Sam and Eric react to their role in Simon's death?
5. What does Jack steal from Ralph's boys?

EXAM PRACTICE
Using one of the 'Key Quotations to Learn', write a paragraph analysing the way Golding presents the boys' violence.

You must be able to: understand what happens towards the end of the novel.

How does Piggy change?

Without his glasses, Piggy becomes braver – he says that he'll demand them back, appealing to Jack's sense of **morality**. Although he's often stood up with the conch, this is the first time he truly shows bravery.

As they get to the tribe, Piggy is afraid but continues. He's helpless without his glasses, reliant on Ralph, and still determined to abide by the rules of the conch and hold others to them as well: 'Which is better – to have rules and agree, or to hunt and kill?'

Roger launches a rock from a cliff; the rock hits Piggy, killing him instantly. His body, like Simon's, is swallowed by the sea.

What happens to Ralph?

Following Piggy's death, Ralph is hunted by the tribe. Although Sam and Eric warn him about the hunt, they tell Roger where Ralph is hiding. He's rescued just in time, by the arrival of the officer as the boys catch up to him on the beach.

What does the officer represent?

For the boys, the officer means rescue – ironically, the fire set by Jack's tribe has raged so out of control it signalled his passing ship. The officer is also a symbol of society and civilisation returning, the order that the boys have been lacking. But he doesn't understand what has happened on the island.

What about the other boys?

Roger is responsible for killing Piggy. When Ralph and Piggy go to Jack's camp at the beginning of Chapter 11, Roger throws stones at them (as he did at Henry in Chapter 4). Then, he deliberately, even joyously, uses the tree trunk to launch a rock that kills Piggy. He 'sharpens a stick at both ends', and tortures Sam and Eric into joining the tribe and betraying Ralph.

Jack fights Ralph and shows no remorse over Piggy's death, but instead leads a hunt to find Ralph. When the officer asks who's in charge, he starts forward but changes his mind.

Key Quotations to Learn

'I don't ask you to be a sport, I'll say, not because you're strong, but because what's right's right. Give me my glasses, I'm going to say – you got to!' (Piggy: Chapter 11)

Then the sea breathed again in a long, slow sigh, the water boiled white and pink over the rock; and when it went, sucking back again, the body of Piggy was gone. (Chapter 11)

'Are there any adults – any grown-ups with you?' ... 'Fun and games,' said the officer. (Chapter 12)

And in the middle of them, with filthy body, matted hair, and unwiped nose, Ralph wept for the end of innocence, the darkness of man's heart, and the fall through the air of the true, wise friend called Piggy. (Chapter 12)

Summary

- Piggy leads the boys to Jack's tribe to ask for his glasses back.
- Ralph and Jack have a physical confrontation.
- Roger launches the rock at Piggy, killing him.
- Sam and Eric are taken by the tribe and tortured to join them.
- The tribe hunt Ralph in a methodical way.
- Ralph tries to escape and discovers a Naval Officer on the beach, who has come to rescue them.

Questions

QUICK TEST
1. How does Piggy demonstrate his bravery?
2. What causes Piggy's death?
3. How does Ralph escape?
4. What is the role of the officer?
5. What happens to Jack at the end?

EXAM PRACTICE
Using one of the 'Key Quotations to Learn', write a paragraph analysing the way characters change in the final chapters.

Narrative Structure

You must be able to: comment on the significance of the way that Golding has structured the novel.

How does Golding increase tension?

Although Golding doesn't specify the length of time spent on the island, he does hint about time passing through the boys' hair growing and the way that they get used to the rhythms of time on the island. The chapters become closer together in time as the book progresses, creating a faster pace and increasing drama.

Golding also uses **echoes** or repeated events to intensify the drama. For example, the three boys in Chapter 1 push a rock from the cliff, and Roger in Chapter 4 throws pebbles at littluns. These events combine in Chapter 11 to become Piggy's death. The deaths of Simon and Piggy also have similar **symbolism** connecting them with nature.

How does Golding use chapters to maintain pace?

Each title suggests what happens in it, for example, 'Beast from Water' is the boys' discussion about the Beast emerging from the sea at night.

The openings of chapters set the mood and **tone**, for example, in Chapter 9, the air is 'ready to explode' as the chapter moves the reader towards Simon's death.

Golding often ends chapters with a dramatic **cliffhanger** or a particularly **emotive** moment, which is then picked up at the beginning of the next chapter. At the start of a chapter, he often moves time or place, for example, at the end of Chapter 4, Ralph leaves the newly-built fire and at the start of Chapter 5, he has called an assembly on the beach to discuss it.

The deaths of the boy with the birthmark and Simon both happen at the end of chapters, yet Piggy's death is in the middle – because it is more of a **catalyst** for Ralph's final isolation.

What is the significance of the ending?

The officer's arrival is perfectly timed – a **deus ex machina** or plot device; the boys are catching up with Ralph and the officer's presence saves him.

In the final pages, Golding draws our attention briefly to Jack, but Roger escapes notice.

Ralph cries at the end, creating a further emotional release for the reader too, who empathises with Ralph and remembers Piggy's death. Yet Golding's final paragraph focusses on the officer, looking out to sea at his ship. This could symbolise the return of society, but also the way that society can turn its back on, and ignore, problems or ideas it can't handle.

Key Quotations to Learn

The first rhythm that they became used to was the slow swing from dawn to quick dusk. (Chapter 4)

A steady current of heated air rose all day from the mountain and was thrust to ten thousand feet; revolving masses of gas piled up the static until the air was ready to explode. (Chapter 9)

The officer … turned away to give them time to pull themselves together; and waited, allowing his eyes to rest on the trim cruiser in the distance. (Chapter 12)

Summary

- Chapter openings establish time and mood, often using **pathetic fallacy**.
- Chapter endings often have cliffhangers or dramatic climaxes, such as deaths or a fight between Ralph and Jack.
- The ending with the officer could symbolise rescue or society's inability to face its responsibilities.
- Golding uses events that mimic or echo those that have come before to intensify the **tension**.

Questions

QUICK TEST
1. How does Golding often begin chapters?
2. How does Golding create drama at the end of chapters?
3. How does Golding use echoing/foreshadowing throughout his novel?

EXAM PRACTICE
Using one of the 'Key Quotations to Learn', write a paragraph analysing the way that Golding creates tension during the novel.

The Island

You must be able to: explore why the island is significant and what it represents.

How is the setting established?

We first see the island through Ralph's eyes. He's excited – 'wizzoh!' – and thinks they'll have great fun. The heat is described as a warm bath, comforting and soothing, and there is plenty of fruit. The boys explore the island and find only sources of fun – Castle Rock, which could become a fort, with **connotations** of adventure, and the beauty of the lagoons in which they swim.

How does the island create a sense of threat?

The plane carrying the boys crash-lands on the island and immediately their presence has damaged the landscape. There is a 'scar' where the plane has landed and the trees have been destroyed, suggesting that this island paradise has been forever tarnished by their presence.

Golding also uses the island to create an **intensifying** sense of fear. The ever-present heat and humidity is oppressive, weighing down on the boys. Frequently, night-time is a source of conflict too; the boys' raids happen at night, they have nightmares about beasts in the darkness, boys sight the parachutist and Simon dies. The heat and dark become things to fear.

Golding also uses the weather on the island, using the pathetic fallacy of the thunderstorms in particular, to suggest increasing anger and conflict between the boys.

What does the island represent?

Golding's island draws on two others. One is *The Coral Island*, a children's novel in which boys have adventures in an island paradise. The second is a reference to the garden of Eden, as the island is beautiful and apparently pure, bathed in warmth and light. Golding's **allegory** uses this Biblical **allusion** to suggest that the boys are, like all mankind, corrupted. Their corruption distorts the island around them – from their initial destruction of it through to their burning parts of it in the fires in Chapters 1 and 12.

Golding also shows the violent, threatening side of nature from the island. At first, this is hinted at through the boys' diarrhoea after eating the fruit – nature making them ill. Golding describes the sea as a **Leviathan**, or monster. The destructive chaos of the lightning storm intensifies the horror of Simon's death.

Key Quotations to Learn

The coral was scribbled in the sea ... Beyond falls and cliffs there was a gash visible in the trees; there were the splintered trunks. (Chapter 1)

The ground beneath them was a bank covered with coarse grass, torn everywhere by the upheavals of fallen trees ... always, almost visible, was the heat. (Chapter 1)

There, where the island petered out in water, was another island; a rock, almost detached, standing like a fort. (Chapter 1)

[About the sea] Then the sleeping leviathan breathed out, the waters rose, the weed streamed, and the water boiled over the table rock with a roar. (Chapter 6)

The sun was bright and danger had faded with the darkness. (Chapter 6)

Summary

- The boys first see the island as fun, exciting and a beautiful paradise.
- Their destruction of the island suggests a Biblical allusion to Eden and the ruin of Paradise by mankind.
- The island also symbolises the violence and indifference of nature.

Questions

QUICK TEST
1. What does the beauty of the island represent?
2. How can the island be interpreted as hellish?
3. How do the boys react to the island?

EXAM PRACTICE
Using one of the 'Key Quotations to Learn', write a paragraph analysing the way that Golding uses the setting to create a sense of uneasiness or fear.

Golding's Background

You must be able to: explain how Golding's background influenced his ideas.

What experiences did Golding have that influenced the novel?

Born in 1911, William Golding had several jobs but perhaps most influential on his writing were working as a teacher and being in the Royal Navy during the Second World War (1939–1945).

He studied Natural Sciences then English Literature at Oxford and then became a teacher of English and Philosophy at a boys' public (fee-paying) school. His own school experiences, and watching the interaction of boys at school, particularly the bullying and tribal inclinations, suggested to him that mankind's nature was inherently difficult and prone to conflict. He once said that he had this thought before writing: 'Wouldn't it be a good idea to write a story about some boys an on island, showing how they would really behave, being boys and not little saints as they usually are in children's books'. In particular, he meant books such as *The Coral Island* in which boys have wonderful adventures, but always behave well and come home safely.

What did Golding say about his motivations for writing the book?

Golding wrote about his religious and psychological reasons for writing the novel. In a lecture about the book he said: 'Man is a fallen being. He is gripped by original sin. His nature is sinful and his state perilous'. Original sin is a Christian idea that suggests everyone is born sinful and everyone has the in-built urge to do immoral things. This is a result of Adam and Eve's disobedience to God in Eden, resulting in mankind having to leave paradise. Golding wrote the novel as an allegory to explore whether mankind is **innately** good or evil – are we born one or the other?

How does Golding explore class divides?

Working at a boys' public school, Golding was primarily teaching well-off, middle- and upper-class students. In the novel, the majority of the boys are from this background, for example, Jack and the choir in their symbolic robes are clearly from a public school. Similarly, Ralph appears to be from a wealthier background. His father is in the navy, his parents take him regularly on holiday with them and he remembers never lacking for anything – an almost **idyllic** existence.

Piggy, however, is working-class. In addition to his physical inequality, he is socially unequal. He tells Ralph he no longer lives with his parents but his aunt ('My dad's dead,' he said quickly, 'and my mum—'). His accent and **non-standard grammar** is mocked in Chapter 1 ('Ass-mar', 'Them fruit'). It's one of the reasons for Jack's dislike, as well as the fact that Piggy manages to be both intelligent and friends with Ralph despite their differences.

Summary

- Golding worked as a teacher at public school, teaching boys English and Philosophy.
- He was interested in the way people behave towards one another and the reasons for their behaviour.
- He believed in evil and in the religious idea of original sin.

Questions

QUICK TEST

1. What influence did Golding's work as a teacher have on his writing?
2. What religious influences did Golding have?
3. How does Golding show Piggy's social inequality?

EXAM PRACTICE

Relating your ideas to Golding's background, write a paragraph explaining how Golding's portrayal of boys was influenced by his own experiences.

You must be able to: understand how the themes of the novel are shaped by the writer's experiences of war and its aftermath.

What experiences did Golding have in the Second World War?

Although he worked mainly as a teacher before the war, during the Second World War Golding was a lieutenant in the Royal Navy. He destroyed German submarines and was involved in shelling Germans from the sea on D-Day, supporting the Allied invasion of France.

Golding said that his experiences affected him deeply: 'When I was young, before the war, I did have some airy-fairy views about man … But I went through the war and that changed me. The war taught me different and a lot of others like me'. Golding was horrified by his wartime experiences and the destruction caused by both sides. He was deeply troubled by the mass casualties, particularly the American bombings of Hiroshima and Nagasaki in Japan.

How did Golding's experiences influence his writing of *Lord of the Flies*?

When, in Chapter 2, Jack says 'We're English, and the English are best at everything', it's laden with authorial irony as Golding doubted the British rationale for what they had done in the war. He's also warning about the dangers of **jingoism**, which is extreme and uncritical patriotism.

Ralph and Jack represent different forms of leadership: Ralph is democratically elected as leader; Jack eventually seizes power – he is a **totalitarian** leader. In the Second World War Germany's leader (Adolf Hitler) was a totalitarian leader. The leaders of most of the Allied countries, e.g. Britain's Winston Churchill, were democratically elected. He also explores **democracy** through the conch and its destruction.

What effect did the Cold War have on the novel?

In the 1950s, there was tension between Russia and America as they increased their stockpile of nuclear weapons. Each country felt threatened, so increased their weapons further. This was called 'the Cold War' because there was no actual fighting, but lots of political arguments, threats and propaganda. Fear of 'mutually assured destruction' because of nuclear war was widespread and people practised 'duck and cover' drills, instructing them what to do if an attack occurred. In the novel, the boys are being evacuated (as children were in the Second World War) and Piggy overhears the pilot talk about an 'atom bomb' before they crash.

Summary

- Golding served in the Royal Navy during the Second World War, witnessing atrocities.
- He came to doubt that 'the end justifies the means' in wartime.
- During the 1950s, the threat of nuclear war was prominent.
- The conflict between the boys echoes the conflict between democracy and totalitarianism in Europe in the 1940s and 1950s.

Questions

QUICK TEST
1. How did Golding's experiences of the Second World War influence the themes he explores in the novel?
2. How was Golding influenced by ideas about British values?
3. How does the story of the novel draw on fears about nuclear war?

EXAM PRACTICE
When Ralph and Piggy discover the conch, Ralph says 'I'll give the conch to the next person to speak. He can hold it when he's speaking'. Relating this idea to the historical context, write a paragraph explaining how the boys can be considered representative of the conflict in mid-twentieth century Europe.

Literary Adventures and Boys' Fiction

You must be able to: explain how Golding's literary experiences influenced his writing.

How was Golding influenced by other stories?

Golding was influenced by *The Coral Island*, *Swallows and Amazons* and *Treasure Island*. These are all classic novels boys read when Golding was a child. In his novel, the boys and the officer relate their experiences directly to *The Coral Island*.

Golding also borrows names from *The Coral Island*, 'Jack' is the most knowledgeable and becomes leader, 'Ralph' is his second-in-command and 'Peterkin' is helpful but timid (Piggy's role). By swapping the two main characters, Jack and Ralph, Golding is **subverting** expectations that readers have about what makes a good leader.

In *Swallows and Amazons*, set in the Lake District, children camp, sail and explore. In *Treasure Island* and *The Coral Island*, the main characters have more unusual exotic adventures but they are always rescued and come home safely.

How does Golding subvert other fiction?

Golding subverts these other novels because while the children in them have adventures and come home safely, in his novels the children are genuinely at risk or even die. In the novels that are Golding's influences, the stories are told with glamour and excitement but there is no glamour in *Lord of the Flies* and the excitement is scary and horror-filled. There are also external **antagonists** or threats in classic boys' adventure stories, particularly violent pirates, but in *Lord of the Flies* the boys are their own enemies.

How does Golding use these fictions in his own work?

Referring to *The Coral Island* in his novel, Golding is drawing a direct comparison for his readers, who would be familiar with these novels. The ironic comparison of these stories would highlight the horrors his characters are experiencing. The boys themselves know the novels and name them during an assembly. Then, the officer at the end refers to *The Coral Island* when he meets Ralph. After the fear and tragedy Ralph has witnessed, to call the activities 'fun and games' and a make-believe war makes the officer seem hopelessly out of touch and naive about the nature of humanity.

Key Quotations to Learn

'It's like in a book.' At once there was a clamour. 'Treasure Island–' 'Swallows and Amazons–' 'Coral Island–' (Ralph: Chapter 1)

The officer grinned cheerfully at Ralph. 'We saw your smoke. What have you been doing? Having a war or something?' Ralph nodded. The officer inspected the little scarecrow in front of him. (Chapter 12)

The officer nodded helpfully. 'I know. Jolly good show. Like the Coral Island.' Ralph looked at him dumbly. For a moment he had a fleeting picture of the strange glamour that had once invested the beaches. (Chapter 12)

Summary

- Golding was influenced by the carefree, fun adventure books *The Coral Island* and *Treasure Island*.
- His characters also know these stories, which shape their expectations.
- Allusions, or references to, the plots and characters of other novels emphasise the horrors the boys experience because of their difference to these original stories.

Questions

QUICK TEST
1. Which children's novels influenced Golding's writing?
2. What's the difference between those novels' **protagonists** and the boys in *Lord of the Flies*?
3. How does referring to these novels create irony?

EXAM PRACTICE
Using one of the 'Key Quotations to Learn', write a paragraph analysing the way that Golding subverts his literary influences.

Ralph

You must be able to: analyse how Ralph is presented in the novel.

How does Golding show the changes in Ralph?

Golding's **bildungsroman** (meaning a story about growing up) shows Ralph lose his innocence – as most of Golding's **third-person narrative** focusses on him, he is the protagonist. At first, he's immature, pretend 'machine-gunning' Piggy and delighted there aren't any 'grown-ups' so they can have fun. The conch is a fun toy, although Ralph quickly respects it as the symbol of democracy Piggy recognises it can be. In Chapter 1, Ralph innocently thinks his father on leave will rescue them. He eventually values thought and intelligence more than fun and games, and sees Piggy as a better friend than Jack as a result.

He struggles with his memory and keeping the idea of the signal fire as his priority, suggesting that everyone is **susceptible** to the **dehumanising** effects of losing civilisation.

How does Ralph lose his innocence?

His conflict with Jack **exacerbates** Ralph's difficulties because he comes to understand that Jack hates him and that Jack behaves this way because he dislikes not being in charge, but he can't work out what to do about it and so learns about his own helplessness.

Ralph also experiences violence, participating in the tribal mock-hunt, hurting Robert. He's a part of Simon's murder but is willing to take responsibility and to try and understand his behaviour.

How good a leader is he?

He's voted leader because he has **gravitas**. He's able to **synthesise** ideas and information – taking Piggy's intelligence, Simon's kindness and Jack's dynamism – and apply them when needed. He's diplomatic but firm, insisting that the boys listen to him and focus on rescue. Yet, these skills don't stop the boys turning on him and it is Jack's fire that ultimately attracts the ship that rescues them.

Key Quotations to Learn

… he might make a boxer, as far as width and heaviness of shoulders went, but there was a mildness about his mouth and eyes that proclaimed no devil. (Chapter 1)

With a convulsion of the mind, Ralph discovered dirt and decay … (Chapter 5)

'There was that – that bloody dance. There was lightning and thunder and rain. We was scared!' 'I wasn't scared,' said Ralph slowly, 'I was – I don't know what I was' (Chapter 10)

And in the middle of them, with filthy body, matted hair, and unwiped nose, Ralph wept for the end of innocence, the darkness of man's heart, and the fall through the air of the true, wise friend called Piggy. (Chapter 12)

Summary

- Ralph is initially childlike and innocent.
- He is voted leader and takes the role seriously.
- He tries to look after others and work towards rescue.
- By the end, he's alone, hunted by the others until the officer arrives.

Sample Analysis

Ralph is presented as almost angelic at first with 'fair hair', 'a golden body' and his 'eyes that proclaimed no devil'. As the novel progresses, his physical condition – like all the boys – deteriorates. His hair grows long and his skin is 'scurfy with brine'. These **adjectives** symbolise the deterioration of morality and civilisation on the island, but also have connotations of religious allegory as they represent the fallen angel, the fall of mankind. Ralph remains disheartened by his appearance, rather than embracing it like some of the other boys, suggesting that he always, at heart, remains civilised.

Questions

QUICK TEST
1. How is Ralph presented as immature at the beginning of the novel?
2. Why is Ralph voted leader?
3. How does Ralph demonstrate his leadership skills?
4. What happens to Ralph's memory?

EXAM PRACTICE
Using one of the 'Key Quotations to Learn', write a paragraph analysing the way that Ralph's maturity is presented throughout the novel.

You must be able to: analyse how Jack is presented in the novel.

How do readers' views of Jack change through the novel?

Jack, the leader of the choir, at first appears arrogant – 'I ought to be chief … because I'm chapter chorister and head boy. I can sing C sharp' – showing his naivety. For Jack, their isolation is an adventure. Because Jack fails to kill the pig the first time, he becomes obsessed with hunting to show his authority.

As Jack becomes more savage, the gap widens between him and Ralph. Jack ignores the need for rescue, another example of his lack of mature understanding. He's part of Simon's murder but refuses to acknowledge it and celebrates when Piggy dies. He also instructs the boys to hunt Ralph.

The final time we see Jack, he stands back – just one of the rest of the boys with his red hair and tattered black cap – and lets Ralph take responsibility for everything that has happened.

What does Jack represent?

Jack **embodies** what happens without the civilising influence of society – we become savages with **dictatorial** rule, tribal groups, beliefs in myth (like the Beast) and ritualised violence. Golding uses Jack as a foil to Ralph, highlighting their leadership differences. Ironically, it's Jack's hunters who set the fire that eventually leads to their rescue when it burns out of control.

What kind of a leader is Jack?

Jack is an authoritative leader, ruling through fear and bullying. He divides the group, telling them they can 'hunt and feast and have fun', ignoring the dangers and their need for rescue. He becomes 'Chief', losing his own name and echoing childish games. He masks his identity with mud as camouflage and orders the other boys to assault one another to prove his control.

Key Quotations to Learn

'We'll have rules!' he cried excitedly. 'Lots of rules! Then when anyone breaks 'em–' 'Whee-oh!' (Jack: Chapter 1)

Jack, faced at once with too many awful implications, ducked away from them. (Chapter 4)

'Use a littlun,' said Jack, and everybody laughed. (Chapter 6)

'I'm not going to play any longer. Not with you.' (Jack: Chapter 8)

The chief was sitting there, naked to the waist, his face blocked out in white and red. (Chapter 10)

Summary

- Jack is naive, seeing the island as an adventure and a game.
- He creates conflict with Ralph to divide the boys.
- His obsession with hunting demonstrates his reversion to tribal savagery.
- He glories in death – first Piggy's, then hunting Ralph.
- At the end, he stands back and becomes a child again, letting Ralph take responsibility.

Sample Analysis

Through Jack, Golding explores the problems of leadership. Jack excitedly shouts that 'We've got to have rules and obey them. After all, we're not savages. We're English, and the English are best at everything'. His repetition of 'English' indicates that he values the democratic way. Yet, ironically, he focusses on the need to 'obey' the rules and 'savages' are exactly what the boys become. Because Jack is proud to be English but ultimately ends up leading through bullying and violence rather than democracy, Golding could be commenting on the way that Britain tries to present itself as democratic but often resorts to these tactics to get what it wants.

Questions

QUICK TEST
1. What ideas about leadership does Jack represent?
2. What is significant about Jack's change in appearance?
3. What are Jack's relationships with Piggy and Ralph like?
4. Does Golding have any sympathy for Jack?

EXAM PRACTICE
Using one or more of the 'Key Quotations to Learn', write a paragraph analysing how Golding presents Jack as a symbol of **authoritarian** leadership.

You must be able to: analyse how Piggy is presented.

What is Piggy like?

Piggy's intelligent and quick-thinking. He recognises the conch and suggests Ralph use it to call a meeting. Physically, he doesn't fit in, which leads to bullying. He's fat, has asthma and is from a lower social class, as represented in his non-standard grammar. He lacks confidence at first but gains more confidence with the conch and his friendship with Ralph. He trusts quickly, telling Ralph his nickname – but is **forthright** when Ralph betrays that trust and tells the other boys.

What does Piggy represent?

Piggy represents intelligence; he knows they should make a list of boys, realises that no grown-ups know where they are and explains how to use the conch. His glasses are a symbol of his intelligence and hope – a testament to mankind's scientific understanding, they're used to light the fires but they become a symbol of conflict too, when Jack first breaks and then steals them. Although he's intelligent – 'What intelligence had been shown was traceable to Piggy' – he lacks the physical presence, charisma and social class of most leaders.

He's closely associated with democracy as he insists on the importance of the conch and adhering to its rules. This gives him courage to ask Jack for his glasses. Ultimately, Piggy has (a perhaps naive) faith that people will eventually do the right thing.

How do the boys respond to Piggy?

Many of the boys bully or belittle Piggy because he is different. Jack resents him for several reasons. First, his developing friendship with Ralph pushes Jack to one side. Second, Jack can't understand the value others place on Piggy, as he can't see past his physical and social inequality.

Ralph develops a close friendship with Piggy. Although he initially tries to avoid him, disliking what he sees, he comes to respect and appreciate Piggy's brains and manner. He sometimes privately finds him amusing, but it's warmly affectionate rather than dismissive. By the end, it is the 'true, wise friend called Piggy' that Ralph weeps for.

Key Quotations to Learn

'I was the only boy in our school what had asthma,' (Piggy: Chapter 1)

'What are we? Humans? Or animals? Or savages? What's grown-ups going to think?' (Piggy: Chapter 5)

'Life,' said Piggy expansively, 'is scientific, that's what it is. In a year or two when the war's over they'll be travelling to Mars and back.' (Chapter 5)

Piggy could think. He could go step by step inside that fat head of his, only Piggy was no chief. But Piggy, for all his ludicrous body, had brains. (Chapter 5)

'Which is better – to have rules and agree, or to hunt and kill?' (Piggy: Chapter 11)

Summary

- Piggy is physically and socially unequal.
- He represents intelligence and, through his glasses, scientific understanding and civilisation.
- Other boys sometimes bully Piggy but Ralph comes to value his intelligence.
- Piggy's death is blunt and brutal, and leaves Ralph alone.

Sample Analysis

Roger pushes the rock that kills Piggy. Golding's description of Piggy's death is blunt and cold – 'stuff came out and turned red' - using **colloquial language** that symbolises the destruction of intelligence on the island. He further describes limbs twitching 'like a pig's after it has been killed', the animalistic **simile** linking Piggy with his namesake but also suggesting that he is the victim of a successful hunt.

Questions

QUICK TEST
1. How does Ralph's attitude towards Piggy change?
2. What symbols are associated with Piggy?
3. How does Jack see Piggy?
4. How does Piggy die?

EXAM PRACTICE
Using one of the 'Key Quotations to Learn', write a paragraph analysing how Piggy represents intellectual thinking.

You must be able to: analyse the significance of Simon in the novel.

How is Simon presented as slightly different?

Simon is in the choir when they arrive. He faints in the heat – a common occurrence, as Jack's sarcastic response shows. It shows he's different, seemingly weaker, but this first impression changes as the reader gets to know Simon. He's kind and thoughtful, getting the littluns fruit when most of the big'uns ignore them, and building shelters.

He dislikes conflict and disappears when others argue, finding solitude and peace in the forest – he is the only boy who seems unafraid of it.

How is Simon connected to the Beast?

Simon's shy and doesn't like speaking in assemblies, making it difficult to explain his ideas about the Beast. He can only say 'maybe it's only us', but the boys don't understand that they are the danger on the island: from themselves and the fear they feel.

In the forest with the pig's head, Simon hallucinates that it's the Beast speaking to him: 'You knew, didn't you? I'm part of you?' He loses his innocence, understanding that evil is part of humanity, but continues to tell the others so they stop being afraid.

How does Simon die?

Trying to tell the boys the truth, Simon stumbles into their tribal celebration after killing the pig. In their bloodlust, exacerbated by the thunder-storm and darkness, the boys mistake him for the Beast and beat him to death.

How is Simon associated with religion?

Simon can be interpreted as a prophet, or even a Christ-like figure. He tells Ralph that he'll get back and Simon is the only boy who realises the truth of the Beast. He dies trying to tell the others and save them from themselves. When he seeks solitude, there are religious connotations, making the forest sound and smell church-like: 'candle-buds', 'their scent like incense'. When Simon dies, he's dressed in light and taken by the sea, symbolising nature reclaiming and honouring him.

Key Quotations to Learn

Simon found for them the fruit they could not reach, pulled off the choicest from up in the foliage, passed them back down to the endless, outstretched hands. (Chapter 3)

However Simon thought of the beast, there rose before his inward sight the picture of a human at once heroic and sick. (Chapter 6)

'You'll get back to where you came from,' (Simon: Chapter 7)

The water rose farther and dressed Simon's coarse hair with brightness. The line of his cheek silvered and the turn of his shoulder became sculptured marble. (Chapter 9)

Summary

- Simon is in the choir, then he becomes friends with Ralph.
- The other boys think he's strange but he's often very kind and thoughtful.
- He realises the truth of the Beast, that it's the potential evil in the boys.
- He's killed by the boys who mistake him for the Beast during a frenzied ritual.

Sample Analysis

Simon's empathy is significant. He finds the body of the parachutist but instead of running away, '[h]e saw how pitilessly the layers of rubber and canvas held together the poor body that should be rotting away'. The descriptive 'pitilessly' and 'poor' emphasise Simon's sympathetic, kind response. He isn't disgusted by the 'rotting' like many of the boys would be but instead steps forward and tries to help, freeing the body so it can drift out to sea and become one with nature again.

Questions

QUICK TEST
1. Who is Simon with at the beginning?
2. How does Simon show his kindness?
3. What is Simon's connection with the Beast?
4. How does Simon die?

EXAM PRACTICE
Using one of the 'Key Quotations to Learn', write a paragraph analysing the way that Simon is associated with religion.

You must be able to: analyse how Roger is presented.

What is Roger like?

Roger is 'furtive' and secretive. He's a loner at first and doesn't seem part of any group at the beginning, although it is Roger who suggests voting for a chief.

He quickly attaches himself to Jack and the hunters, where he has an opportunity to express his violent nature. He becomes Jack's second-in-command and makes a role for himself as torturer and enforcer.

How does Roger create fear and tension?

Roger's violence escalates quickly. In Chapter 4, he throws stones at Henry. He throws to miss, remembering the rules of society, but his actions are menacing. During the hunt, he is the most violent boy, thrusting the spear 'right up her ass' in a disturbing symbolic raping of the creature before mounting her head on a stick.

Later, Roger 'sharpens a stick at both ends' for Ralph, rather than the sow's head, and throws the rock that kills Piggy. He tortures Sam and Eric into joining Jack's tribe and into giving up Ralph's location.

How does Roger compare with the other boys?

Roger is less **ambiguous** because he seems interested in violence and savagery from the beginning. He is arguably the most 'evil' of the boys. With the reference to the 'law' in Chapter 4, Golding suggests he's previously had some trouble at home, but on the island, he quickly moves away from social constraints.

Contextually, Roger represents people who take pleasure in their persecution of others when sanctioned by authority, such as Jack as Chief.

Key Quotations to Learn

Round the squatting child was the protection of parents and school and policemen and the law. Roger's arm was conditioned by a civilisation that knew nothing of him and was in ruins. (Chapter 4)

Roger, with a sense of delirious abandonment, leaned all his weight on the lever. (Chapter 11)

Roger advanced upon them as one wielding a nameless authority. (Chapter 11)

'You don't know Roger. He's a terror.' 'And the chief – they're both' '– terrors –' '– only Roger –' (Sam and Eric: Chapter 12)

Summary

- Roger becomes one of the most violent hunters.
- Roger acts as torturer and enforcer, particularly regarding Sam and Eric.
- Roger 'sharpens a stick' to hunt Ralph.
- Roger delights in violence and is responsible for Piggy's death.

Sample Analysis

Roger is a figure of terror in the novel. Initially he is described as a 'slight, furtive boy whom no one knew, who kept to himself with an inner intensity of avoidance and secrecy'. Golding's **semantic field** of secrecy suggests that there is something hidden in Roger, which emerges through the novel. Later, he sees Ralph as a 'shock of hair' and Piggy as a 'bag of fat', dehumanising them and refusing to acknowledge their humanity so that he can torture them.

Questions

QUICK TEST
1. What is Roger like at the beginning?
2. How does Roger's relationship with Jack develop?
3. What violent actions does Roger carry out?
4. Who does Roger represent?

EXAM PRACTICE
Using one of the 'Key Quotations to Learn', write a paragraph analysing the way that Golding associates Roger with violence.

The Beast

You must be able to: explore the representation of the Beast.

What versions of the Beast are there?

The Beast has several incarnations, each representing something different about the boys and their fear.

At first, the Beast is the boys' nightmares, experienced in the dark, and in 'Beast from Water', they fear it emerges from the sea as they sleep. They might also mistake the forest's creepers for a snake-like monster, intensifying their fear.

Then, in 'Beast from Air' the dead parachutist arrives and gets tangled in the trees. Each time there's a breeze it moves, simulating breathing. This is what frightens Sam and Eric, driving the boys from the mountain, and that is what Simon sees.

The Beast is also the pig's head, mounted on a stick and 'speaking' to Simon. This connects the beast with the devil, the Lord of the Flies, as Simon realises the true nature of the Beast. Simon himself becomes 'the beast' when he stumbles into the boys' ritual and they kill him.

How does the Beast influence the storyline?

During the assembly in Chapter 5, fear of the Beast creates conflict as the boys have different impressions of what it might be, Piggy and Ralph try to rationalise it, while Jack uses it as an opportunity to hunt. Ralph also experiences difficulties in leadership when it seems the boys believe in the **supernatural** because of their fears.

Sam and Eric's discovery of the parachutist, not stopping to investigate and understand it, means the boys avoid the mountain and make Ralph feel more hopeless.

After a successful hunt, Jack regresses to pre-Christian rituals and makes the boys leave the pig's head as a sacrificial offering to the Beast, but it then embodies the Beast to Simon.

What does the Beast mean when it speaks to Simon?

When Simon hears the pig's head 'talking', he realises the Beast is the boys' own capacity for evil. He had begun to understand this before, but had not been able to fully express his thoughts.

Key Quotations to Learn

'Now he says it was a beastie.' (Piggy: Chapter 2)

'... they talk – not only the littluns, but my hunters sometimes – talk of a thing, a dark thing, a beast, some sort of animal.' (Jack: Chapter 5)

'What I mean is ... maybe it's only us.' (Simon: Chapter 5)

'You knew, didn't you? I'm part of you? Close, close, close! I'm the reason why it's no go? Why things are what they are?' (Beast: Chapter 8)

'No! How could we – kill – it?' (Jack: Chapter 10)

Summary

- There are different incarnations of the Beast throughout the novel, all representing fear and evil.
- The dead parachutist is the evil of the outside world coming to the island.
- The Beast can't be killed because it's the fear and evil inside the boys themselves.

Sample Analysis

The Beast appears in different forms, increasing tension and fear. At first, it's a 'beastie', the suffix making it seem less consequential, even child-like. This changes with the monstrous symbol of the parachutist giving the beast physical form, with its 'ruin of a face', suggesting the ugliness and deformity of death. This is further echoed in the pig's head 'grinning' at Simon, then Ralph, mocking them both.

Questions

QUICK TEST
1. What different forms does the Beast take?
2. How does the Beast affect Ralph?
3. What is Jack's response to the Beast?

EXAM PRACTICE
Using one of the 'Key Quotations to Learn', write a paragraph analysing the way the Beast changes form during the novel.

Sam and Eric

You must be able to: analyse the way Sam and Eric are presented.

What are Sam and Eric like?

As identical twins, Sam and Eric act together, and gradually lose their individual identities as the novel continues. They are cheerful, bright and bubbly boys but they are not leaders. They follow Jack and Ralph, eventually choosing Ralph's side when Jack leaves. Later, they are frightened when Roger kills Piggy and harms them, so they change sides again and re-join Jack's hunters to protect themselves. At the end of the novel, they are hunting Ralph, albeit reluctantly.

How do they change?

The twins do everything together and come to be seen as one person by the other boys. They speak as one, finishing each other's sentences, representing their unity. Their name changes to 'Samneric', suggesting it doesn't matter who's who. This change represents the way that many of the boys lose their individual identities while they are on the island, because they forget or change the social conditioning that has made them the people they are, and instead become animals and savages.

What do Sam and Eric represent?

Sam and Eric follow the strongest leader – for a while that's Ralph but it changes to Jack and Roger, particularly when Roger begins to torture them. Although they tell Ralph what's happening with the hunters, they also betray Ralph so the hunters can find him. Through the twins, Golding explores collaborators in wartime who change allegiance to save themselves.

Key Quotations to Learn

… the eye was shocked and incredulous at such cheery duplication. They breathed together, they grinned together, they were chunky and vital. (Chapter 1)

The twins shared their identical laughter, then remembered the darkness and other things and glanced round uneasily. (Chapter 6)

Samneric were part of the tribe now. (Chapter 12)

'Listen, Ralph. Never mind what's sense. That's gone –' (Eric: Chapter 12)

Summary

- Sam and Eric are identical twins who do everything together.
- They begin as hunters, then support Ralph after Jack separates the groups.
- When Jack hunts Ralph, they first help him and give him food. After Jack and Roger torture them, they give away Ralph's hiding place.

Sample Analysis

When they first arrive, the boys are 'grinning and panting at Ralph like dogs'. The **verbs** are cheerful and friendly, while the simile suggests they will be loyal. Describing them as 'like dogs' also implies that they are more like pets, willing followers not leaders. They stay loyal to Ralph, helping him hide and giving him food. When Roger and Jack threaten and hurt them, they turn on Ralph and give away his hiding place.

Questions

QUICK TEST
1. How are the boys first described?
2. Who do the boys support?
3. How does their name change?
4. What happens at the end?

EXAM PRACTICE
Using one of the 'Key Quotations to Learn', write a paragraph analysing how Golding presents Sam and Eric's identities.

The Littluns

You must be able to: analyse the way the littluns are presented.

Who are the littluns?

These are the youngest – and as their name suggests – and smallest boys. Unlike the older boys, who are named as individuals, the littluns are seen mostly as a group. A few littluns are identified directly – the boy with the birthmark, Percival Wemyss Madison, Henry and Johnny.

The littluns don't do much and are left to look after themselves. They play, eat and bathe then sleep. At night, they have nightmares about 'beasties' coming for them.

How do the littluns interact with the older boys?

The littluns interact with the older boys mostly at assemblies, where they enjoy the ritual and similarity to home experiences at school. They giggle, whisper and disrupt, because they don't know what's happening but they are also reliant on the older boys.

The older boys differ; Simon looks after the littluns, getting them fruit. Ralph also takes his leadership seriously. But the others pay them little attention except to dismiss them as annoying.

What do the littluns represent?

The littluns frequently represent society's tendency to ignore the most vulnerable. The 'boy with the birthmark' disappears after the fire in Chapter 1; he isn't named, which suggests his lack of importance, but he haunts the later chapters. Other boys, such as Percival Wemyss Madison, also lose their names and they all become the 'littluns', a homogeneous identity of the vulnerable in society who most need protection and don't get it.

By the end, the littluns are malnourished and near starvation, with distended bellies. There is also the boy with the birthmark, who is forgotten in Ralph's tally of 'two' bodies, and there are probably other littluns nobody has noticed go missing. Percival Wemyss Madison, who chants his address like an 'incantation' to keep him safe, forgets everything including his name by the time the officer arrives.

Key Quotations to Learn

'That little 'un that had a mark on his face – where is – he now? I tell you I don't see him.' (Piggy: Chapter 2)

They obeyed the summons of the conch, partly because Ralph blew it, and he was big enough to be a link with the adult world of authority. (Chapter 3)

'They talk and scream. The littluns. Even some of the others. As if –'
'As if it wasn't a good island.' (Ralph, then Simon: Chapter 3)

Percival Wemyss Madison, of the Vicarage, Harcourt St. Anthony, lying in the long grass, was living through circumstances in which the incantation of his address was powerless to help him. (Chapter 5)

Other boys were appearing now, tiny tots some of them, brown, with the distended bellies of small savages. (Chapter 12)

Summary

- The littluns are mostly unnamed, treated as one group.
- They are often ignored by the older boys as unimportant or annoying.
- They symbolise the forgotten but most vulnerable members of society.

Sample Analysis

Jack's casual 'use a littlun' suggests the uncaring nature of the older boys towards them. Although Ralph and Simon look after them, building shelters and finding food, they don't behave in a grown-up manner towards them. The name 'littluns' puts them all together, removing their individuality – they are beneath the notice of most older boys, as the lowest group in society is often ignored.

Questions

QUICK TEST
1. Who are the main littluns?
2. What does calling them 'littluns' represent?
3. How do the littluns contribute to the fear on the island?
4. What happens to Percival Wemyss Madison?
5. What happens to the boy with the birthmark?

EXAM PRACTICE
Using one of the 'Key Quotations to Learn', write a paragraph analysing the role of the littluns in the novel.

Power and Leadership

You must be able to: analyse how Golding presents different types of leadership.

What kinds of leadership are there?

Jack and Ralph's leadership represents the conflict between democracy and dictatorship. Ralph listens to the others and they're able to give him opinions whereas Jack exerts total control.

What is Jack's leadership like?

Jack thinks he should lead because he's 'head boy' and can 'sing C sharp'. Although being head boy suggests he already has some authority, the second reason suggests he doesn't understand what true leadership involves as well as highlighting how young Jack is – only very young boys can sing a C sharp. Although he takes control of the hunters, he resents Ralph's authority and that Ralph listens to other boys, such as Piggy, equally.

Jack has an authoritarian leadership style. He later calls another vote and leaves when he doesn't like the outcome. Jack becomes a tribal 'chief' and paints his face to make himself seem more important. He is more interested in control than leading; he's excited by the prospect of punishment, and eventually uses fear and pain as ways to keep control, for example, tying up Wilfred to beat him.

What is Ralph's leadership like?

The boys choose Ralph as chief because of his attitude. Ralph is logical and deliberate, taking his leadership role seriously. He stays focussed on the important things – the rescue fire and building shelters – even when he would rather be doing something more fun.

He develops an understanding of people, for example, how to get attention at assemblies and that blowing the conch when they won't come back undermines his authority (Chapter 5).

Who has more power?

Power shifts back and forth; Ralph is leader at first and for a while the others accept him, but the boys turn towards a dictatorship when Jack seems to promise them fun and adventure, which are things that they want.

Key Quotations to Learn

What intelligence had been shown was traceable to Piggy while the most obvious leader was Jack. But there was a stillness about Ralph as he sat that marked him out. (Chapter 1)

'We'll have rules!' he cried excitedly. 'Lots of rules! Then when anyone breaks 'em –' 'Whee-oh!' (Jack: Chapter 2)

Power lay in the brown swell of his [Jack's] forearms: authority sat on his shoulder and chattered in his ear like an ape. (Chapter 9)

Summary

- Golding explores the conflict of democracy and dictatorship.
- Ralph is democratic: logical, rational and fair.
- Jack is dictatorship: controlling, often violent and unpredictable.

Sample Analysis

The conch symbolises the conflict between Ralph's democracy and Jack's dictatorship. Blown by Ralph, the other boys follow its rules: the **declarative** 'I got the conch' is a repeated statement on an individual's right to speak and be heard. When the conch is 'exploded into a thousand white fragments and ceased to exist', the violent verbs show the decisive end of democracy as Jack completely takes over.

Questions

QUICK TEST
1. What kinds of leadership are there?
2. What kind of a leader is Ralph?
3. What kind of a leader is Jack?
4. What symbols are associated with leadership?

EXAM PRACTICE
Using one of the 'Key Quotations to Learn', write a paragraph analysing the conflict between democracy and dictatorship.

Civilisation and Society

You must be able to: analyse the way that ideas about society are presented.

What are civilisation and society?

Golding explores the way that society works. He questions what makes humanity different to animals and asks whether people are capable of overcoming original sin. Readers see what could happen when society's rules and moral teachings are stripped away.

How does Ralph present civilisation?

In addition to his role as democratic leader, Ralph is aware that his clothing and cleanliness are markers of civilisation. In Chapter 1, he removes his school uniform to swim, symbolically eliminating the identifying marks of civilisation – the literally unifying clothes that mark him as part of a community.

He later realises how dirty the boys are and how ragged their clothing is – the outward signs of civilisation deteriorating, just as their social attitudes are deteriorating.

How do Jack and Roger present civilisation?

Both boys give up civilised behaviour and revert to savagery. In Jack's case, he uses mud as war-paint and becomes a 'chief', sitting above the others and commanding them. For Roger, the loss of civilisation means the loss of rules that mean he can't hurt other people and, instead, give him licence to glory in violence.

How does Piggy present civilisation?

For Piggy, 'life is scientific'. His constant references to civilisation are connected with intelligence: tracking time with a sundial, or building planes or a ship. He is also insistent on the importance of the conch as a sign of rules, society and community working together.

How does the officer represent society?

The arrival of the officer symbolises the return of civilisation to the island. At first, Ralph sees the pieces making up the man's uniform (a link to Ralph's school uniform) and then the whole man.

Ironically, although the officer represents society, it is as part of the navy – an organisation that functions through hierarchy and violence. He is a reminder that the adult society outside the island is still engaged in the way of living that brought the boys to the island in the first place – this is a comment on the fact that society is perhaps not so 'civilised' after all.

Key Quotations to Learn

This toy of voting was almost as pleasing as the conch. (Chapter 1)

'Things are breaking up. I don't understand why. We began well; we were happy. And then –' (Ralph: Chapter 5)

With a convulsion of the mind, Ralph discovered dirt and decay. (Chapter 5)

He saw white drill, **epaulettes**, a revolver, a row of gilt buttons down the front of a uniform. (Chapter 12)

Summary

- Ralph witnesses the boys' loss of civilisation through the breakdown of their community and the shedding of their clothing.
- Jack and Roger lose their sense of civilisation and revert to violent savagery.
- The officer represents the return of society, but maybe society isn't so civilised.

Sample Analysis

The conch is a symbol of civilisation, and it enables the boys to listen to each other and abide by rules. Golding describes Piggy holding 'the talisman, the fragile, shining beauty of the shell' (Chapter 11). The **noun** 'talisman' gives the conch a sense of magic or luck, while the adjectives 'fragile, shining' create an impression of beauty and peace. But the conch is also easily broken, just like the **veneer** of civilisation, which breaks, leaving the boys as violent savages.

Questions

QUICK TEST
1. How does Ralph see the deterioration of society?
2. How do Jack and Roger show the loss of civilisation?
3. What does Piggy see as civilisation?
4. What does the officer represent?

EXAM PRACTICE
Using one of the 'Key Quotations to Learn', write a paragraph analysing the way that Golding presents the deterioration of civilisation on the island.

Death and Violence

You must be able to: analyse how the theme of violence is presented in the novel.

Which deaths occur in the novel?

Although boys are probably killed in the plane crash (and the pilot), the first character's death in the book is the boy with the birthmark, following the first fire that gets out of control – this is an accidental death. After this, Simon is beaten to death by the boys following a hunt and Piggy is killed by Roger's rock. There is also the death of the parachutist, who lands on the island, and the constant threat of death, at first from the island and nature, and then increasingly from other boys.

Why do the boys resort to violence?

As the laws of society are forgotten, the boys descend into savagery and animalistic behaviour. However, unlike animals, the boys take pleasure in the excitement of violence, celebrating it in tribal rituals.

Ralph's experience in these rituals demonstrates the underlying potential for violence in all the boys – he joins in despite being, in most other ways, a moral and responsible leader. Yet he, too, participates in Simon's death. He also physically fights Jack in Chapter 11, an echo of the way that nations will fight one another despite claiming to be essentially peaceful.

How does the violence change?

At first, the violence is playful or pretend. Jack fails to kill a pig because of the 'enormity of the knife descending and cutting into living flesh' and Roger throws stones avoiding Henry because he remembers the **censure** of society. But by the time Jack and his hunters succeed, the boys viciously thrust spears into the pig and celebrate their victory.

As hunters, the violence is restricted to a condoned place – the need to hunt and find meat – mirroring the way that in society violence is viewed as being acceptable in some instances, such as in war or when combating criminality. However, violence becomes uncontrolled and spills out into murder.

Key Quotations to Learn

[Jack] snatched his knife out of the sheath and slammed it into a tree trunk. Next time there would be no mercy. (Chapter 1)

Ralph too was fighting to get near, to get a handful of that brown, vulnerable flesh. The desire to squeeze and hurt was over-mastering. (Chapter 7)

The sticks fell and the mouth of the new circle crunched and screamed. The beast was on its knees in the centre, its arms folded over its face. (Chapter 9)

Summary

- Deaths in the novel become progressively more deliberate.
- At first, violence is pretend and playful, but it becomes more real and dangerous.
- The boys become more violent as the rules of civilisation are forgotten.

Sample Analysis

When Ralph and Piggy first meet, Ralph 'returned as a fighter-plane, with wings swept back, and machine-gunned Piggy'. The play-acting metaphor is a stark contrast with the real, deadly violence that takes place later in the novel but is also a reminder that the children have so far been shielded from the real violence of the adult world.

Questions

QUICK TEST
1. Who dies in the novel and how?
2. How is violence controlled early in the novel?
3. How does Ralph react to violence?

EXAM PRACTICE
Using one of the 'Key Quotations to Learn', write a paragraph analysing the way that violence develops on the island.

You must be able to: analyse how Golding presents ideas about fear in the novel.

How does fear affect the boys?

Early on, most of the boys don't express fear directly. Golding alludes to fear in Ralph and Piggy's conversation when Piggy says that nobody knows where they are and Ralph refuses to think about it, because he is afraid.

The boys express fear in the assembly when discussing the Beast and their nightmares, the blackness exacerbating their fear. They argue over what they should be afraid of rather than how to stop being afraid.

Ralph worries that fear stops the boys acting rationally – he thinks that with the fear of the Beast they forget that the signal fire is all-important. Ralph recognises the power of fear to distort behaviour.

Fear becomes paralysing, literally when they see the parachutist, and figuratively when they stop trying to be rescued because they can no longer set a signal fire on the mountain. Fear stops most of the boys, except Simon, seeing things rationally: they run from the parachutist in terror. Only Simon is able to master his fear and see the reality of what the parachutist is.

How do the boys deal with their fear?

They try to ignore their fear. When it's inescapable, fear turns to either **bravado** or violence. For Jack, the boys' fear becomes an opportunity to seize power. At the beginning, he demonstrates bravery by promising to hunt the Beast – his action makes them less afraid – but Jack then uses the idea of the Beast to keep the hunters in line.

What should they be afraid of?

Golding's characters repeatedly say that they should be afraid of the unknown or of themselves. Simon's statement 'Maybe it's only us' could also be interpreted as suggesting that they should be more afraid of their own fear and the detrimental effect it has on them. The idea of the Beast comes to mean more because they are afraid of it.

Key Quotations to Learn

'We've got to talk about this fear and decide there's nothing in it.' (Ralph: Chapter 5)

To Ralph, seated, this seemed the breaking up of sanity. Fear, beasts, no general agreement that the fire was all-important ... (Chapter 5)

'Fear can't hurt you any more than a dream.' (Jack: Chapter 5)

'I know there isn't no beast – not with claws and all that I mean – but I know there isn't no fear either.' (Piggy: Chapter 5)

'I'm scared ... Not of the beast. I mean I'm scared of that too. But nobody else understands about the fire.' (Ralph: Chapter 9)

Summary

- The boys talk about what they should be afraid of, instead of how to deal with their fear.
- The boys often express fear through bravado or violence.
- Fear stops them behaving in rational and logical ways.
- Golding suggests they should be more afraid of fear than the Beast.

Sample Analysis

As Ralph approaches the parachutist, not knowing what it is, he demonstrates courage: 'He bound himself together with his will, fused his fear and loathing into a hatred, and stood up'. The verb 'fused' suggests it takes force of will for him to decide to overcome his fear and move forward, but the noun 'hatred' is a violent, unsettling word, which suggests that he is deliberately transforming his fear into aggression.

Questions

QUICK TEST
1. How does Jack handle his fear?
2. What does Ralph think of fear?
3. What does Golding suggest they should be afraid of?

EXAM PRACTICE
Using one of the 'Key Quotations to Learn', write a paragraph analysing the way that fear affects the boys in the novel.

You must be able to: analyse the way that Golding uses religious allusions in his novel.

What are the religious concepts in the novel?

The novel has allegorical aspects considering good and evil. It also explores people in the middle who are influenced by those around them, as Golding saw people change during the Second World War. Golding believed he witnessed evil during the war, and through characters such as Jack and Roger, he explores whether people are born evil or can become evil, depending on what happens to them.

Golding also explores pre-Christian religion in the way that Jack leads the hunters to worship the Beast and leaves it the sacrifice of the pig's head to appease it and protect them.

Who is the Lord of the Flies?

The Greek for Satan is 'Beelzebub', which translates to 'Lord of the Flies'. Flies also feed on dead animals, as Simon sees on the pig's head. Simon's hallucination brings together concepts of death, religion, sin and punishment.

What is original sin?

In the Biblical story of Adam and Eve, humanity suffers original sin because Adam and Eve tasted the fruit of the tree of knowledge, against God's instructions, and 'fell' or were cast out from Eden. This means every human is born sinful and needs Christ's forgiveness to enter heaven. In the novel, this is the reason that the boys are doomed to tear each other apart with violence – mankind is inherently violent and sinful, and is only held back from this behaviour by social conditioning.

How does Simon fit in?

Some of Golding's most overt religious **imagery** concerns Simon, a Christ-like martyr figure. He seeks solitude, but ends up speaking with the devil (as Jesus did, wandering in the desert to prepare for his task). Simon also spends time in church-like clearings and ministers to the littluns as Jesus did to children around him. Trying to tell the truth to the boys, Simon too is crucified by those who don't know or understand him.

Key Quotations to Learn

'Snake-thing' (Littlun: Chapter 2)

'This head is for the beast. It's a gift.' (Jack: Chapter 8)

The usual brightness was gone from his [Simon's] eyes and he walked with a sort of glum determination like an old man. (Chapter 8)

Jack, painted and garlanded, sat there like an idol. (Chapter 9)

Summary

- The novel allegorically explores concepts of good and evil present in mankind.
- 'Beelzebub' is a name for the devil and also means Lord of the Flies, which manifests in the pig's head.
- There are also pre-Christian religious ideas, including sacrifice and worshipping of idols.
- Simon is a Christ-like figure in the novel.

Sample Analysis

The island can be paradise or hell. As Simon sits in front of the pig's head the clouds 'squeezed … this close, tormenting heat'. The oppressive verbs hold connotations of hellish punishment and torture while the 'obscene thing grinned' in front of him, characterising the head as a satanic figure enjoying the torture of humanity.

Questions

QUICK TEST
1. Who is the Lord of the Flies?
2. What is original sin?
3. What pre-Christian ideas are associated with Jack?
4. What Christ-like imagery is associated with Simon?

EXAM PRACTICE
Using one of the 'Key Quotations to Learn', write a paragraph analysing the way that Golding presents religion in the novel.

Innocence

You must be able to: analyse the way Golding shows the loss of innocence in the boys.

What is innocence?

Innocence is either a lack of guilt, or lack of experience, understanding or wisdom. Golding writes a bildungsroman exploring the ways that the boys grow up and lose their childish innocence. They come to understand the depths that humanity is capable of and commit some terrible crimes themselves.

What represents a change in Ralph's innocence?

For Ralph, his father and his attitude to rescue are important. His innocence means he has a childish naive attitude when they crash – that his father will come for him. Ralph dreams of home periodically, but as an idyllic childhood holiday with full cupboards, ponies to ride and the protection of his parents. Gradually, though, he ceases to believe this and has trouble remembering that they need a signal fire at all as he loses hope of rescue. In Chapter 10, Ralph laughs sarcastically when Piggy tells him 'You're still Chief', because he recognises the pointlessness of assigning leaders when they have no hope of effecting a rescue.

The final presence of the naval officer, a symbol of paternal rescue, is an enormous let-down as he not only doesn't understand what the boys have been through, but literally turns his back on Ralph instead of offering comfort.

Where else is innocence lost?

Many of the boys transition from childish play to violence and murder. They also have an impact on the island; Simon's church-like haven in the jungle is corrupted so that the next time he visits, the pig's head is staked in the middle and appears to him as the devil.

What about the adult world?

The outside world also loses its innocence. The boys were being evacuated from an atomic war and the officer who rescues them has detoured from hunting the enemy. While they might be escaping the horrors of the island, the boys are being taken back to an unstable, war-torn adult world.

'[Daddy] He's a commander in the Navy. When he gets leave he'll come and rescue us. What's your father?' (Ralph: Chapter 1)

'Grown-ups know things,' said Piggy. 'They ain't afraid of the dark. They'd meet and have tea and discuss.' (Chapter 5)

'And what happened? What's grown-ups goin' to think? Young Simon was murdered.' (Piggy: Chapter 11)

Ralph wept for the end of innocence, the darkness of man's heart, and the fall through the air of the true, wise friend called Piggy. (Chapter 12)

Summary

- Ralph's change of attitude towards his father and rescue shows his loss of innocence.
- The boys lose their childhood innocence on the island and corrupt the island as well.
- The adult world returns with the officer, but it too has lost its innocence.

Sample Analysis

After Simon's death, Ralph confesses to Piggy: 'I'm frightened. Of us. I want to go home. Oh God, I want to go home'. His desire reminds the reader how young all the boys are and contrasts with the first chapter when he is confident that his father will rescue them 'when he gets leave', and he is in no hurry. Here, the **fragmented sentences** and **exclamation** 'oh God' reinforces the desperation and sorrow he feels over Simon's death, having realised the horrors of which the boys are capable.

Questions

QUICK TEST
1. What symbolises Ralph's loss of innocence?
2. How do the boys' change of attitude show their loss of innocence?
3. How does the officer suggest loss of innocence?

EXAM PRACTICE
Using one of the 'Key Quotations to Learn', write a paragraph analysing the way that Golding mourns the loss of childhood innocence.

Identity

You must be able to: analyse how the theme of identity is presented in the novel.

What is identity?

Identity is the characteristics and personality of an individual; Golding explores the ways identity is created through society and community, and the way that it can be altered through names, actions and appearance.

How does Jack's identity change?

Jack is introduced as 'Merridew', leader of the choir. He calls the others 'kids' names' and wants to keep his more grown-up status. But he becomes 'Jack' instead and, as he becomes obsessed with hunting, his identity further changes. He uses 'dazzle paint' to change his face, which camouflages him from the pigs but also makes him appear strangely different, unlike a 'civilised' boy.

As he becomes more savage, Jack becomes known as 'Chief', losing his name but taking on a title. He's also 'painted and garlanded', changing his appearance to a more tribal, savage identity.

How does appearance contribute to identity?

The boys' clothing deteriorates quickly and their uniform, a symbol of community and civilisation, falls apart – some by their doing as they take it off and some through use and wear.

Jack isn't the only one to use camouflage; others adopt the mud-masks and become 'striped brown, black and red' (Chapter 12) rather than wearing their uniform. Their appearance is what makes the officer question their nationality, as the littluns have the 'distended bellies of savages'. The officer himself is also introduced through his appearance, the crisp military uniform with its white symbolising the purity grown-up society likes to think it has.

How does Ralph's memory contribute to his identity?

Ralph has increasing trouble remembering why the signal fire is important. He describes a 'flicker' or 'curtain' in his mind closing off his thoughts; he is beginning to lose his own memory of who he is and what is important, as well as the language with which to express it.

This is taken even further through the character of Percival Wemyss Madison, who in Chapter 5 recites his name and address as an 'incantation' of safety but by Chapter 12, he can't remember either.

Key Quotations to Learn

[Jack] looked in astonishment, no longer at himself but at an awesome stranger. (Chapter 4)

They understood only too well the liberation into savagery that the concealing paint brought. 'Well, we won't be painted,' said Ralph, 'because we aren't savages.' (Chapter 11)

Most, he was beginning to dread the curtain that might waver in his brain, blacking out the sense of danger, making a simpleton of him. (Chapter 12)

Summary

- Many of the boys lose their identities; Jack's deterioration is the most pronounced.
- The increasing camouflage and changing appearance reflect the boys' changing identities.
- Ralph has trouble with his memory, losing his connection with home.

Sample Analysis

Names change through the novel as the boys' identities alter. 'Piggy' is dehumanised from the start, confessing his nickname and finding this used against him – his name focusses on his weight, which socially defines him, but also foreshadows his 'hunting' by Roger. We never learn Piggy's real name, making the most intelligent boy seem less important. Jack changes name the most, from the pseudo-adult 'Merridew' to 'Jack' and finally 'Chief' as he changes his identity from head choir-boy to a tribal leader.

Questions

QUICK TEST
1. What does Jack's changing name suggest about his identity?
2. How do the boys' appearances change with their identities?
3. How does Ralph's memory suggest his loss of identity?

EXAM PRACTICE
Using one of the 'Key Quotations to Learn', write a paragraph analysing the way Golding represents the loss of the boys' identities.

Friendship

You must be able to: analyse how the friendships in the novel change.

How does Jack and Ralph's friendship change?

Jack and Ralph share a shy companionship at first; although Ralph's voted as chief, he's diplomatic and offers Jack control of the choir. When they explore with Simon, the three of them are happy, excited with 'a kind of glamour' around them.

Jack becomes frustrated when Ralph listens to others as much as him, then further frustrated when he's not given an opportunity to lead his way and Ralph values the fire over his hunting. When he lets the signal fire out Jack, 'faced at once with too many awful implications, ducked away from them', first attacking Piggy to deflect attention from his mistake, then refusing to acknowledge what he's done wrong. Instead he offers an apology designed to get the others on his side, angering Ralph with this 'verbal trick'.

When Jack loses a second vote, he leaves humiliated, although Ralph calls him back.

How does Ralph and Piggy's friendship change?

Ralph tries to ignore Piggy. After he's voted chief, he chooses Jack and Simon to explore the island with – partly because of Piggy's physical unfitness and partly because he'd rather have fun with the others. Piggy confides his nickname, and Ralph disloyally shares it, and it becomes the only name we know. He realises his mistake, but argues 'better Piggy than Fatty'.

Ralph consistently stands up for Piggy, both in his role as leader and as friend. He considers Piggy's feelings, and looks after him despite Jack's disapproval.

Ralph comes to respect Piggy's intelligence and logical approach. He realises that 'I can't think. Not like Piggy'. When Jack's tribe has disappeared, the two become closer and discuss ways to get rescued. After Piggy's glasses are stolen, leaving him blind, he trusts Ralph to lead him up to demand them back from Jack but during the confrontation Ralph attacks Jack, leaving Piggy vulnerable.

Through the two friendships, Golding explores what it is to be friends – loyalty, comfort, a similarity of thinking – and how important it is to choose friends wisely.

Key Quotations to Learn

By the time the pile was built, they [Ralph and Jack] were on different sides of a high barrier. (Chapter 4)

'... we can start again and be careful about things like the fire.' A picture of three boys walking along the bright beach flitted through his mind. 'And be happy.' (Piggy: Chapter 5)

'No, I'm not. I just think you'll get back all right.' For a moment nothing more was said. And then they suddenly smiled at each other. (Simon, to Ralph: Chapter 7)

... a true, wise friend called Piggy. (Chapter 12)

Summary

- Jack and Ralph begin as friends, but their relationship deteriorates.
- Jack is jealous of Piggy's friendship with Ralph and Ralph's position as leader.
- They disagree on the importance of the signal fire compared with hunting.
- Ralph increasingly recognises Piggy's value in his intelligence and loyalty.

Sample Analysis

Ralph confronts Jack (in Chapter 7) as Jack sneers at him when they're climbing the mountain. Asking 'why do you hate me?' Ralph exposes the unspoken conflict between them that has driven apart the group. His question is described as 'indecent', suggesting that it should remain unspoken. Instead, Ralph openly addresses Jack's antagonism, which stems from his jealousy of Ralph's power over the group and Ralph's friendship with Piggy.

Questions

QUICK TEST
1. What makes Jack's friendship with Ralph decline?
2. What is Ralph's attitude towards Piggy like at first?
3. Why does Ralph change his attitude to Piggy?

EXAM PRACTICE
Using one of the 'Key Quotations to Learn', write a paragraph analysing the way the theme of friendship is explored in the novel.

Tips and Assessment Objectives

You must be able to: understand how to approach the exam question and meet the requirements of the mark scheme.

Quick tips

- You will get a choice of two questions. Do the one that best matches your knowledge, the quotations you have learned and the things you have revised.

- Make sure you know what the question is asking you. Underline key words and pay particular attention to the bullet point prompts that come with the question.

- You should spend about 45 minutes on your *Lord of the Flies* response. Allow yourself five minutes to plan your answer so there is some structure to your essay.

- All your paragraphs should contain a clear idea, a relevant reference to the text (ideally a quotation) and analysis of how Golding conveys the idea. Whenever possible, you should link your comments to the novel's context.

- It can sometimes help, after each paragraph, to quickly re-read the question to keep yourself focussed on the exam task.

- Keep your writing concise. If you waste time 'waffling' you won't be able to include the full range of analysis and understand what the mark scheme requires.

- It is a good idea to remember what the mark scheme is asking of you …

AO1: Understand and respond to the text (12 marks)

This is all about coming up with a range of points that match the question, supporting your ideas with references from the novel and writing your essay in a mature, academic style.

Lower	Middle	Higher
The essay has some good ideas that are mostly relevant. Some quotations and references are used to support the ideas.	A clear essay that always focusses on the exam question. Quotations and references support ideas effectively. The response refers to different points of the text.	A convincing, well-structured essay that answers the question fully. Quotations and references are well-chosen and integrated into sentences. The response covers the whole text (not everything, but ideas from across the text rather than just focussing on one or two sections).

AO2: Analysing effects of Golding's language, form and structure (12 marks)

You need to comment on how specific words, language techniques, sentence structures, **dialogue** or the narrative structure allow Golding to get his ideas across to the reader. This could simply be something about a character or a larger idea he is exploring through the text. To achieve this, you will need to have learned good quotations to analyse.

Lower	Middle	Higher
Identification of some different methods used by Golding to convey meaning. Some subject terminology.	Explanation of Golding's different methods. Clear understanding of the effects of these methods. Accurate use of subject terminology.	Analysis of the full range of Golding's methods. Thorough exploration of the effects of these methods. Accurate range of subject terminology.

AO3: Understand the relationship between the novel and its contexts (6 marks)

For this part of the mark scheme, you need to show your understanding of how the characters or Golding's ideas relate to the time when he was writing (1954) or when the novel was set.

Lower	Middle	Higher
Some awareness of how ideas in the novel link to its context.	References to relevant aspects of context show a clear understanding.	Exploration is linked to specific aspects of the novel's contexts to show detailed understanding.

AO4: Written accuracy (4 marks)

You need to use accurate vocabulary, expression, punctuation and spelling. Although it's only four marks, this could make the difference between a lower or higher grade.

Lower	Middle	Higher
Reasonable level of accuracy. Errors do not get in the way of the essay making sense.	Good level of accuracy. Vocabulary and sentences help to keep ideas clear.	Consistent high level of accuracy. Vocabulary and sentences are used to make ideas clear and precise.

Practice Questions

1. How does Golding present Jack in *Lord of the Flies*?

   Write about:
   - the ways Jack behaves through the novel
   - how Golding presents Jack through the text.

2. How does Golding use Simon to explore ideas about kindness in *Lord of the Flies*?

   Write about:
   - how Golding presents Simon
   - how Golding uses Simon to explore some of his ideas.

3. Piggy is described as a 'true, wise friend'. Explore how far you agree with this statement.

   Write about:
   - how Golding presents the character of Piggy
   - how Golding uses Piggy to present some of his ideas.

4. Who do you think is the most powerful character in *Lord of the Flies*?

   Write about:
   - how different characters behave in ways that make them seem powerful
   - how Golding presents some characters as being more powerful than others.

5. Early in the novel, Roger is described as a boy who 'kept to himself with avoidance and secrecy'. How does Golding use Roger to explore ideas about violence?

   Write about:
   - the way that Golding presents Roger
   - the way that Golding uses Roger to explore some of his ideas.

6. How does Golding present the relationship between Jack and Ralph?

   Write about:
   - the way that their relationship changes through the novel
   - the way that Golding presents their relationship by the ways that he writes.

7. 'Ralph underestimates the importance of Piggy until the end'. Explore how far you agree with this statement.

   Write about:
   - the way the relationship between Piggy and Ralph changes
   - the way that Golding presents their relationship by the ways that he writes.

8. How does Golding present the littluns in *Lord of the Flies*?

   Write about:
   - how Golding presents the littluns
   - how Golding uses the littluns to explore some of his ideas.

9. At the end of the novel, the boys are rescued but 'Ralph wept for the end of innocence'. What do you think is the importance of the ending of *Lord of the Flies*?

   Write about:
   - how the ending of the novel presents important ideas
   - how Golding presents those ideas in the ways that he writes.

10. How does Golding present ideas about leadership in *Lord of the Flies*?

    Write about:

    - how Golding uses the boys to explore ideas about leadership
    - how Golding presents leadership in the way that he writes.

11. At the end of the novel, Ralph wept for 'the darkness of man's heart'. How does Golding present 'the darkness of man's heart' in *Lord of the Flies*?

    Write about:

    - some of the ideas about savagery and cruelty
    - the methods that Golding uses to explore his ideas.

12. How does Golding present death in *Lord of the Flies*?

    Write about:

    - what some of the ideas about death are
    - how Golding presents these ideas by the ways he writes.

13. 'We've got to have rules and obey them. After all, we're not savages.' How does Golding present ideas about civilisation?

    Write about:

    - what some of Golding's ideas about civilisation are
    - how he presents these in the way that he writes.

14. Simon suggests: 'Maybe there is a beast … maybe it's only us.' What do you think is the importance of the Beast in *Lord of the Flies*?

    Write about:

    - the way that Golding presents the Beast
    - the way that Golding uses the Beast to explore some of his ideas.

15. Piggy says 'Life … is scientific … I know there isn't no beast … but I know there isn't no fear, either … Unless we get frightened of people'.

    Explore the ways that Golding presents ideas about fear in the novel.

    Write about:

    - what some of the ideas about fear are
    - the ways that Golding presents these in his writing.

16. How does Golding present ideas about good and evil in *Lord of the Flies*?

    Write about:

    - the ideas Golding has about the contrast of good and evil
    - how he presents these ideas in the way that he writes.

Planning a Character Question Response

You must be able to: understand what a character-based question is asking you and prepare your response.

How might an exam question on character be phrased?

A typical character question will usually look like this:

How and why does Ralph change in *Lord of the Flies*?

Write about:

- what Ralph does, and the reasons for his actions
- the way Golding presents Ralph by the way he writes.   [30 marks + 4 AO4 marks]

How do I work out what to do?

Work out the focus of the question – in this case, it is about the way Ralph changes. A good way to think about character questions is often to ask 'why is this character significant and what happens to make them significant?' and address the question that way.

'How' and 'why' are important elements. For AO1, you need to show understanding of the way that Ralph changes, what happens to make him change and the way that he responds to change.

For AO2, the word 'how' means you need to analyse the way that Golding's use of language, structure and form contribute to the reader's understanding of Ralph's developing character. Ideally, you should have quoted evidence, but you can *make clear reference* to specific parts of the novel if necessary.

You also need to remember to link your answer to context to achieve AO3 marks and write accurately to gain the four AO4 marks for spelling, punctuation and grammar.

How do I plan my essay?

You have approximately 45 minutes to answer this question.

Although it doesn't seem long, spending the first five minutes writing a quick plan helps to focus your thoughts and produce a well-structured essay, which is an essential part of AO1.

Try to think of five or six ideas. Each of these ideas can become a paragraph. If possible, add a quick reminder of a quote or context you could write about, but focus on getting the main paragraph ideas down.

You can plan however you find most useful: a list, spider-diagram or flow chart. Once you have your ideas, take a moment to check which order you want to write them in.

Look at the example on the opposite page.

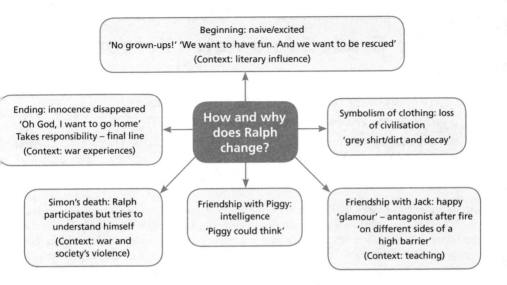

Beginning: naive/excited
'No grown-ups!' 'We want to have fun. And we want to be rescued'
(Context: literary influence)

Ending: innocence disappeared
'Oh God, I want to go home'
Takes responsibility – final line
(Context: war experiences)

How and why does Ralph change?

Symbolism of clothing: loss of civilisation
'grey shirt/dirt and decay'

Simon's death: Ralph participates but tries to understand himself
(Context: war and society's violence)

Friendship with Piggy: intelligence
'Piggy could think'

Friendship with Jack: happy 'glamour' – antagonist after fire
'on different sides of a high barrier'
(Context: teaching)

Summary

- Make sure you understand the focus of the question. (AO1)
- Analyse the way the writer conveys ideas through use of language, structure and form. (AO2)
- Link ideas to social and historical context. (AO3)

Questions

QUICK TEST
1. What key skills do you need to include in your answer?
2. What timings should you use?
3. Why is planning important?

EXAM PRACTICE
Plan a response to the following exam question:
How and why does Jack change in *Lord of the Flies*? Write about:
- what Jack does, and the reasons for his actions
- the way Golding presents Jack by the way he writes.
[30 marks + 4 AO4 marks]

Grade 5 Annotated Response

How and why does Ralph change in *Lord of the Flies*? Write about:

- what Ralph does, and the reasons for his actions
- the way Golding presents Ralph by the way he writes.

[30 marks + 4 AO4 marks]

At the beginning of the novel, Ralph is naive and innocent. He is excited by the thought that there are 'no grown-ups', which means they can do as they like on an island that is like paradise. He thinks his father will rescue them 'when he gets leave', which suggests he is innocent (1) and thinks there's no hurry to be rescued. He doesn't understand the seriousness of their situation but hopes it will be an adventure, like 'The Coral Island' and 'Treasure Island', books which inspired Golding to tell a story of what he thought would really happen (2).

Ralph's relationships show the changes in his character (3). At first, he's closest to Jack – he offers him control of the hunters and they are described as having a 'kind of glamour' around them and Simon. The word 'glamour' suggests a magic spell cast over them, to make everything appear perfect (4). The conflict between them gets worse when Jack lets the signal fire out to focus on hunting. Ralph punishes him – this is shown with the quote that there is a 'high barrier' between them that they can't break down (5). This might be Golding's way of exploring the difficulties of war as he could be suggesting that staying focussed on peace is harder than getting swept up in the violence of war (6).

Golding uses a **motif** of Ralph's clothing (7), which shows a gradual change as Ralph loses his civilisation and his innocence. At the beginning of the story, he wears a grey school uniform which shows he is part of a community and of society. When he takes off his uniform to go swimming in Chapter 1, it shows that it is easy to 'take off' society and its rules. He describes it as 'strangely pleasing' to put the uniform on again. The verb 'pleasing' shows how much Ralph needs order and civilisation at the start. This changes later. 'With a convulsion of the mind, Ralph discovered dirt and decay'. The **alliteration** emphasises the unpleasantness of his clothing and appearance, and the violent noun 'convulsion' indicates the severity of his dislike (8) and that he has changed without realising it (9).

Ralph also changes his attitude towards violence. At the start, he is described as 'machine-gunning Piggy', which reminds the reader about the violent adult world and hints at the potential for violence that is inside the children. During the mock-hunt with Robert, Ralph is more violent. A quote showing this is 'The desire to squeeze and hurt was over-mastering'. The violent verbs suggest that he's overcome and not in control because something inside him is forcing him to behave differently. Golding is suggesting that all people are born with original sin and that they all have the capacity for evil (10). The reader is most shocked when Ralph is a part of Simon's death. Ralph is different because, unlike most of the boys, he admits what he has done and tells Piggy 'I wasn't scared,' said

Ralph slowly. 'I was - I don't know what I was.' The **adverb** implies that he is trying to work out his response and understand it, so he can work out why he behaved that way. He doesn't look for excuses for his behaviour (11).

Finally, Ralph's friendship with Piggy also demonstrates the way he changes. Although at the beginning he tries to ignore Piggy, by the end he relies on him totally and appreciates his intelligence and logic. At the end, Ralph doesn't weep for Simon, or Jack or himself, but for the 'true, wise friend called Piggy' (12).

1. Clear ideas being discussed, with textual evidence, although not much is done with the quotation. AO1/AO2

2. Reference to literary context shows awareness of Golding's influences. AO3

3. Clearly structured, focussed on the question, with topic sentences to guide the reader. AO1

4. Developing analysis of the language methods used. AO2

5. Focus on the question and how this is structurally presented. Golding's structure could be more explicitly addressed. AO1/AO2

6. Clearly linked to historical context, although a little generalised and 'bolted on' at the end. AO3

7. Close reference to language and structure through the technical vocabulary. AO2

8. Short, precise quotations analysed; some terminology. AO2

9. Refers to change at the end of the paragraph to keep focussed. AO1

10. Embedded context, although could be applied in more detail to the language used. AO3

11. Exploring the effect on the reader, could link back to question. AO1

12. Clear though slightly rushed conclusion. Writing is clear and competent. AO1/AO4

> ## Questions
>
> EXAM PRACTICE
> Choose a paragraph of this essay. Read it through a few times then try to improve it. You might:
> * Replace a reference with a quotation.
> * Analyse a quotation in more depth, including terminology.
> * Improve the range of analysis of methods.
> * Improve the expression or sophistication of the vocabulary.
> * Connect more context to the analysis.

Grade 7+ Annotated Response

> A proportion of the best top-band answers will be awarded Grade 8 or Grade 9.
> To achieve this, you should aim for a sophisticated, fluid and nuanced response that displays flair and originality.

How and why does Ralph change in *Lord of the Flies*? Write about:

- what Ralph does, and the reasons for his actions
- the way Golding presents Ralph by the way he writes.   [30 marks + 4 AO4 marks]

Ralph loses the innocence he has in Chapter 1. Like the other boys, he commits unthinkable acts of savagery, but unlike them, he tries to understand his nature. Through Ralph, Golding explores the concept that civilisation and society are fragile and easily broken veneers covering the darkness of human nature, and that all growing up is a loss of innocence (1) as we enter the corrupt adult world Golding experienced during the Second World War (2).

Ralph's loyalties change as he matures. At first, he's in awe of 'Merridew'; Jack's use of his surname shows he's slightly older, more in tune with the adult world in which Ralph has faith. A 'kind of glamour' lies across the explorers, the noun creating an impression of magic and fantasy covering the Edenic island (3). Despite this, the 'scar' and fallen trees suggest a dark underside being hidden, both a reference to original sin that runs through the novel, and a contrast to the adventure books that inspired Golding – 'The Coral Island' and 'Treasure Island' – where everyone gets home safely. Ralph is initially too naive to distinguish between fiction and reality (4).

Golding shows the shift in Ralph's allegiances from Jack to Piggy as Ralph matures (5). Ralph's anger over Jack's inability to understand the importance of the fire leaves a 'high barrier' between them, which is impossible to overcome. Instead, Ralph increasingly values Piggy: 'Piggy could think. He could go step by step inside that fat head of his, only Piggy was no chief'. The **derogatory** *noun 'fat head' is strangely affectionate and although Ralph knows Piggy's limitations, he values what Piggy can offer. Golding describes Piggy as 'no chief', neither a democratic leader like Ralph nor a 'chief' or dictator like Jack, but he can think clearly when others can't. Ralph's evolving friendships also represent his growing up, drawing on Golding's observations from his time as a public school teacher when he watched students' changing friendships. As a child, Ralph values 'Merridew', who is arrogant and charismatic, and ignores his bullying ways, flattered to be liked. As Ralph matures, he prefers Piggy's loyalty and intelligence, and is less influenced by physical appearance.*

Golding's bildungsroman form shows Ralph's loss of innocence and his change into a leader responsible for others, taking his place in the adult world (6). The adult world is always on the edges of the novel and is symbolised in the dead parachutist and the atomic war, the cause of the children's evacuation, elements which were influenced by the Cold War of the 1950s. Ralph's confidence his father will rescue them is naive, and the officer's arrival later is a poor substitute rescue. Gradually Ralph becomes

used to thinking and considers his moves 'as though he were playing chess', the simile suggesting the
intellectual difficulty of developing his leadership responsibilities (7).

Golding's wartime experiences shook his religious faith. He described the novel as 'mourning the lost
childhood of the world' as Ralph loses his childhood. The officer's arrival symbolises the transition
from child to adult; the officer condescendingly refers to 'fun and games ... like The Coral Island', an
ironic **juxtaposition** as the island's 'shuddering with flame'. Golding's use of personification implies
that nature is horrified by the boys' actions (8).

Golding shows Ralph's developing responsibility through his actions: building shelters rather than
hunting, then trying to accept his part in Simon's death and finally, when the officer asks who's in
charge, Ralph replies 'I am' (9). The adult world has, for Ralph, changed from being populated with
heroes like his father, a place where food and safety is always assured. Instead, it now belongs to the
officer with his revolver, flanked by ratings with machine guns, who symbolise a war more violent
than the boys on the island. The officer, the symbol of the corrupt adult world that Golding explores
with the 'darkness of man's heart', can't offer Ralph any comfort at all as he grieves for the innocence
and childhood he has lost – Golding describes how the officer simply 'turned away ... and waited,
allowing his eyes to rest on the trim cruiser in the distance' (10).

1. Engages with Ralph as a constructed character designed to explore a theme. AO1

2. A brief but relevant link to context. AO3

3. Close language analysis of an embedded quotation. AO2

4. Context is embedded in the paragraph and used to explore Golding's meaning. AO3

5. A continuation of the first point, showing development of ideas. AO1

6. Use of terminology linked with form to develop the argument. AO1/AO2

7. Language analysis including terminology, used to comment on the question, returning
    to ideas of change ('development'). AO1/AO2

8. Analysis of embedded quotation with more complex terminology. AO2

9. Conceptual overview: quick references from throughout the book show a confident
    whole-text understanding. AO1

10. Well-written conclusion with a confident final conclusion. The essay is well structured
    with sophisticated writing throughout. AO1/AO4

Questions

EXAM PRACTICE
Spend 45 minutes writing an answer to the following question.

How and why does Jack change in *Lord of the Flies*? Write about:
*   what Jack does and the reasons for his actions
*   the way Golding presents Jack by the way he writes.

Remember to use the plan you have already prepared.
[30 marks + 4 AO4 marks]

Planning a Theme Question Response

You must be able to: understand what a theme-based question is asking you to do and prepare your response.

How might an exam question on theme be phrased?

A typical theme question will usually look like this:

How does Golding use his island setting to explore ideas about religion and human nature in *Lord of the Flies*? Write about:

- the way Golding presents the island
- how Golding uses the island to explore ideas about religion and human nature.

[30 marks + 4 AO4 marks]

How do I work out what to do?

Work out the focus of the question – in this case, the bullet points offer useful guidance – the main theme is religion, as seen through the symbol of the island.

'How' and 'why' are important elements. For AO1, you need to show understanding of the way the island represents different aspects of religion and the way that nature on the island can be seen to explore human nature.

For AO2, the word 'how' means you need to analyse the way that Golding's use of language, structure and form contributes to the reader's understanding of religion through the island. Ideally, you should have quoted evidence, but you can make *clear reference* to specific parts of the novel if necessary.

You also need to remember to link your answer to context to achieve AO3 marks and write accurately to gain the four AO4 marks for spelling, punctuation and grammar.

How do I plan my essay?

You have approximately 45 minutes to answer this question.

Although it doesn't seem long, spending the first five minutes writing a quick plan helps to focus your thoughts and produce a well-structured essay, which is an essential part of AO1.

Try to think of five or six ideas. Each of these can become a paragraph.

You can plan however you find most useful: a list, spider-diagram or flow chart. Once you have your ideas, take a moment to check which order you want to write them in.

Look at the example on the opposite page.

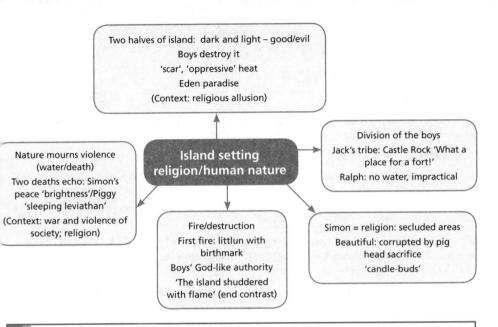

Two halves of island: dark and light – good/evil
Boys destroy it
'scar', 'oppressive' heat
Eden paradise
(Context: religious allusion)

Nature mourns violence (water/death)
Two deaths echo: Simon's peace 'brightness'/Piggy 'sleeping leviathan'
(Context: war and violence of society; religion)

Island setting religion/human nature

Division of the boys
Jack's tribe: Castle Rock 'What a place for a fort!'
Ralph: no water, impractical

Fire/destruction
First fire: littlun with birthmark
Boys' God-like authority
'The island shuddered with flame' (end contrast)

Simon = religion: secluded areas
Beautiful: corrupted by pig head sacrifice
'candle-buds'

Summary

- Make sure you understand the focus of the question. (AO1)
- Analyse the way the writer conveys ideas through use of language, structure and form. (AO2)
- Link ideas to social and historical context. (AO3)

Questions

1. What key skills do you need to include in your answer?
2. What timings should you use?
3. Why is planning important?

EXAM PRACTICE

Plan a response to the following exam question:

Piggy says to Ralph: 'Grown-ups know things ... They ain't afraid of the dark'. How does Golding present ideas about being a grown-up in *Lord of the Flies*? Write about:

- the ideas Golding has about being a grown-up
- how he presents these ideas in the way that he writes.

[30 marks + 4 AO4 marks]

How does Golding use his island setting to explore ideas about religion and human nature in *Lord of the Flies*? Write about:

- the way Golding presents the island
- how Golding uses the island to explore ideas about religion and human nature.

[30 marks + 4 AO4 marks]

The island is often divided into two, which represents the good and evil in the boys' nature. As the novel can be interpreted as a religious allegory (1), Golding uses the island as paradise or Eden and as Hell (2).

*The conflict of good and evil is present from the start as the boys damage the island in their crash (3). 'A long scar smashed into the jungle'. This uses violent language and **sibilance** to describe the way the island is destroyed, the dark side of the boys' nature (4). The island's darkness develops further as it is always too hot and the heat is described as 'almost visible' and 'oppressive'. This language suggests the heat weighs them down and they can't keep their dark side under control. As Golding believed in original sin, he uses this idea to explore the idea that mankind is innately evil (5).*

Golding divides the island into two (6). When the boys go up the mountain, they see the side of paradise and the damaged side where everything is dead. 'Trees, forced by the damp heat, found too little soil for full growth, fell early and decayed'. The language of death suggests the darkness of this side. In comparison, there are other trees that 'reclined against the light'. The verb 'reclined' shows that the other side is peaceful and comfortable (7). The boys divide the island between them when Jack splits the group. Castle Rock is 'like a fort'. Golding uses this simile to create connotations of playfulness and adventure, like in 'The Coral Island' and 'Treasure Island' that influenced Golding. Ralph points out that it is not practical because it has no fresh water and would be dangerous. He knows they would be better elsewhere, which suggests Ralph is a more responsible leader (8).

Simon can be interpreted as a Christ-like figure. He is described with religious imagery and linked with goodness. He is first to find the 'candle-buds' and see their beauty when Ralph and Jack are focussed on fire and food. When Simon goes into the clearing, it is described as beautiful, like Paradise. 'The candle-buds opened their wide white flowers glimmering under the light that pricked down from the first stars'. This quote shows the peace of Simon's island and that it's like Eden. Golding uses images of white light to show that the place is pure, and to remind readers of a church with candles and incense (9). However, this place becomes corrupted when the boys put the pig's head on a stick in the middle of it. Golding does this to suggest that their original sin and violent human natures are destroying Paradise. Golding is also influenced by his experiences in the war, where he saw people do terrible things they wouldn't otherwise have done, leading him to think that mankind is evil, which can be seen in the way such a peaceful place changes into a place linked to death.

Golding uses the island, especially the sea, to guide the reader's impression of the two deaths and the immorality of the other boys (10). When Simon and Piggy die, their bodies are taken by the sea around the island but these are described very differently. Simon's body is 'dressed ... with brightness', using light imagery to show his martyrdom, and mourn in a religious way (11). The boys have not deliberately murdered him (his death was not intentional) but their violent natures caused them to do it. Nature treats Simon's body carefully. In contrast, what happens to Piggy's body is described angrily: 'the sleeping leviathan breathed out, the waters rose, the weed streamed, and the water boiled over the table rock with a roar'. Golding uses vicious language that makes the waves sound angry and unpredictable, like nature is angry with the boys for what they have done.

The religious allegory of the novel can be seen through the way the island is divided into heaven and hell, and the way that the boys, because of the innate evil of human nature, have destroyed it (12).

1. Clear introduction linked to the theme. AO1
2. Context is referred to, though could be explored more. AO3
3. Well organised writing with clear topic sentences to guide the reader. AO1
4. Embedded quotation with terminology, although writing could be developed. AO2
5. Clear use of context, although a little 'bolted-on' at the end. AO3
6. Repeats introduction – avoid directly repeating ideas. AO1
7. Analysis of specific language methods. AO2
8. Brings back to the theme of the question. The sentence is a little awkward and could be more clearly phrased. AO1/4
9. Close analysis of language but the quote could have been more selectively embedded. AO2
10. Using echoed events to explore Golding's use of structure. AO2
11. Analysis of language linked with the theme. AO1/AO2
12. A clear though quick conclusion that links back to the question. Writing is usually clear although there are some long sentences that wander. AO1/AO4

Questions

EXAM PRACTICE
Choose a paragraph of this essay. Read it through a few times then try to improve it. You might:
- Replace a reference with a quotation.
- Analyse a quotation in more depth, including terminology.
- Improve the range of analysis of methods.
- Improve the expression or sophistication of the vocabulary.
- Connect more context to the analysis.

Grade 7+ Annotated Response

How does Golding use his island setting to explore ideas about religion and human nature in *Lord of the Flies*? Write about:

- the way Golding presents the island
- how Golding uses the island to explore ideas about religion and human nature.

[30 marks + 4 AO4 marks]

Through the island setting, Golding explores religious ideas of original sin, paradise and mankind's fall (1). The duality of the island foreshadows the divisions between the boys and within them as the conflict between Ralph's moral focus on rescue clashes with Jack's increasing tribal savagery (2).

The island is described as an idyllic paradise, with beautiful tropical shores, 'feathery' palms, and a 'warm bath' lagoon. But Golding also creates a threatening undertone – the plane crash creates a 'scar smashed into the jungle', the sibilance emphasising the violent destruction, and scars never completely disappear. The 'almost visible' heat is 'oppressive', crushing the boys – a further ominous threat (3). This setting, reminiscent of Eden, reminds a 1950s reader of man's fall, suggesting the darker natures of the boys too are 'almost visible' (4).

Divisions on the island become more extreme (5). On the damaged mountainside there are trees that 'fell early and decayed'. The semantic field of death juxtaposes with other trees, which 'reclined in the light', the verb suggesting peace and comfort while 'light' suggests heaven (6). The boys further create division as the hunters follow Jack to Castle Rock, which is 'like a fort'. The playful, childish simile creates literary allusions to The Coral Island and Treasure Island, where shipwreck is an adventure and everyone gets home safely, but the darkness on the island and the first accidental death of the boy with the birthmark suggest that this will not happen (7).

Golding also uses Simon to explore religion on the island, as he is a Christ-like figure, associated with nature (8). He finds the 'candle-buds' beautiful when Ralph and Jack focus on the practicalities of fire and food. Simon's solitude reveals the island's beauty, like Eden as the 'candle-buds opened their wide white flowers glimmering under the light that pricked down from the first stars'. Golding's use of light and scent is reminiscent of a church with candles and incense. However, this place becomes corrupted as the boys' darker natures emerge (9). Reverting to a pre-Christian tribal religion, the sacrificial pig's head is placed in the clearing, destroying its purity. Here, Golding suggests that religion can become perverted and destructive (10).

Golding also uses the island, especially the symbolism of water, to create an echo between the deaths of Simon and Piggy. Their bodies are taken by the sea in a symbolic cleansing that has connotations of baptism, the ceremony intended to wash away sin. Simon's body is 'dressed ... with brightness', using the light imagery to draw religious associations and suggest his martyrdom. The calm, peaceful tone of this water as it 'softly' moved shows that the boys didn't deliberately murder Simon but are subject to the evil in human nature as a result of original sin: their dark natures have come through. Golding contrasts this with Piggy's death when he uses **zoomorphism** to suggest the angry, destructive nature of the water: 'the sleeping leviathan breathed out, the waters rose, the weed streamed, and the water boiled over the table rock with a roar'. The noise and violent verbs, contrasted with the peaceful slowness of Simon's death, could be interpreted as nature – the paradise they started in – being completely corrupted by their presence, now monstrous itself (11).

Golding's religious allegory explores his grief for the world he saw lost through his wartime experiences, which persuaded him of the reality of original sin (12). The boys on the island, alone and unguided, are unable to prevent themselves falling into violence and destruction. There is also a tremendous sense of anger in the idea that this paradise has at its core a danger – the oppressive heat, the thunder storms and the darkness in which nightmares of the Beast can flourish. This duality also poses the question: when such horrors and original sin exist, how can a Christian god be considered loving? (13).

1. Close connection to themes, unpicking the question. AO1

2. Reference to structural methods. AO2

3. Developed analysis of language, with embedded precise quotation. AO2

4. Confident link to social and religious contexts, linking back to the question. AO3

5. Developing the argument further, a sense of cohesion throughout. AO1

6. Connecting language analysis closely to the theme. AO1/AO2

7. Connections between literary context and the whole novel understanding. AO1/AO3

8. Confidently structured paragraph, linking theme and character. AO1/AO2

9. Developing analysis of structure and the theme. AO1/AO2

10. Brief summation of the paragraph's argument, linking back to the question. AO1

11. Developed analysis of language with literary terminology. AO2

12. Using context at the start of the conclusion to place Golding's ideas. AO3

13. Ending a conclusion with a quotation or question can be a confident way to open out into the wider messages or ideas of the book. AO1/AO4

Questions

EXAM PRACTICE
Spend 45 minutes writing an answer to the following question:
Piggy says to Ralph: 'Grown-ups know things ... They ain't afraid of the dark'. How does Golding present ideas about being a grown-up in *Lord of the Flies*? Write about:
- the ideas Golding has about being a grown-up
- how he presents these ideas in the way that he writes.

Remember to use the plan you have already prepared.
[30 marks + 4 AO4 marks]

Glossary

Adjective – a word that describes a noun.

Adverb – a word that describes a verb.

Allegory – a story with a hidden meaning, usually moral, religious or political.

Alliteration – a series of words beginning with the same sound.

Allusion – a reference to something else, for example, other novels, the Bible.

Ambiguous – open to more than one interpretation.

Animalistic – having the physical or behavioural qualities of an animal.

Antagonist – a character/group of characters in opposition to the protagonist.

Atmosphere – the mood or emotion in a novel.

Authoritarian – enforcing strict obedience to authority rather than individual freedom.

Bildungsroman – a book about children growing up.

Bravado – a show of bravery intended to impress or intimidate.

Catalyst – something that starts an event or chain of reaction.

Censure – to severely disapprove of.

Cliffhanger – ending a chapter with a shock or problem.

Colloquial language – informal, everyday vocabulary.

Conflict – a disagreement or argument.

Connotation – an idea or feeling created by a word, as well as its literal meaning.

Credibility – the quality of being trusted or believed in.

Declarative – a strong statement.

Decorum – appropriate, 'good' behaviour.

Dehumanising – being reduced from human.

Democracy – a system of leadership where members vote and all are represented equally.

Derogatory – critical or disrespectful.

Deus ex machina – an unexpected event saving a hopeless situation, often unrealistically.

Dialogue – speech by characters.

Dictatorial – typical of a ruler with total power.

Echoes – refers to a previous event or similar scene or idea.

Embodies – represents or gives visible form to something.

Emotive – creating or describing strong emotions.

Epaulettes – ornamental shoulder pieces, usually on uniform.

Exacerbates – to make a bad situation or feeling worse.

Exclamation – sudden forceful cry often denoted by an exclamation mark.

Foreshadowing – hint at future events in the novel.

Forthright – direct and outspoken.

Fragmented sentences – very short groups of words that look like sentences but aren't grammatically complete, for example, 'oh no'/'of us'.

Frenzied – wildly excited or uncontrolled.

Gravitas – a quiet seriousness or dignity.

Idyllic – happy, peaceful or picturesque.

Imagery – words used to create a picture in the imagination.

Imperative – an order.

Innate – natural, born with it.

Intensifying – to make more intense or stronger.

Irony – something that seems the opposite of what was expected; deliberately using words that mean the opposite of what is intended.

Jingoism – extreme patriotism, often aggressive.

Juxtaposition – placement of two contrasting things side by side for emphasis.

Leviathan – a sea monster, often Biblical and associated with evil.

Metaphor – a descriptive technique where one thing represents something else.

Morality – an understanding of the distinction between good and evil.

Motif – a repeated series of images or symbols.

Non-standard grammar – not conforming to rules of grammar or vocabulary.

Noun – the name of an object or thing.

Oppressive – harsh or brutal treatment.

Organism – individual life-form, plant or animal.

Parallelism – repeating similar word orders or sentence constructions to emphasise an idea.

Pathetic fallacy – attributing human emotions to weather or nature, often to create a mood.

Petered – to fall off in volume, intensity, size, etc

Pronoun – a word that takes the place of a noun (such as: I, she, them, it).

Protagonist – the main character of a novel.

Rhetorical question – a question asked to create thought rather than to get a specific answer.

Ritualistic – using a pre-determined series of actions or behaviours.

Sadist – Someone who takes pleasure in hurting or humiliating others.

Savage – fierce, violent and uncontrolled. Related to people, uncivilised and primitive.

Semantic field – a series of connected words.

Sibilance – repetition of 's' sounds.

Simile – a descriptive technique, using comparison to say one thing is 'like' or 'as' something else.

Solitude – being alone, though not lonely.

Subvert – undermine through using opposing ideas, to unsettle them.

Supernatural – something beyond scientific understanding or laws of nature.

Susceptible – likely to be influenced by.

Symbolism – when an object or colour represents a specific idea or meaning.

Syndetic structure – using conjunctions (and, because) to create a list.

Synthesise – put different ideas together often to create something else.

Tension – a feeling of anticipation, discomfort or excitement in a novel.

Third-person narrative – A story told by a narrator using third person 'he/she/they'.

Tone – the quality, emotion or mood of writing.

Totalitarian – a dictatorial system of government in which people are completely subservient to the state.

Triadic structure – three related ideas, placed together for emphasis.

Undertones – an underlying quality or feeling.

Veneer – a thin covering to make something more appealing.

Verb – a doing or action word.

Zoomorphism – giving inanimate objects animalistic qualities.

Answers

Pages 4–5

Quick Test

1. Ralph, the leader; Piggy, the intelligent but unattractive boy; Simon, the quiet boy who faints; Jack, leader of the choir and hunters.
2. The boys have been in a plane crash while being evacuated, and have landed on a desert island without any adults.
3. A beastie they think they've seen, although Ralph says it's a nightmare.
4. Jack doesn't like others being in charge, especially those who seem inferior (which Piggy is physically).
5. A part of the island is destroyed and the little boy with the birthmark dies.

Exam Practice

Answers might include exploration of the way that conflict begins between Jack and Ralph but is defused by their agreement to share leadership of the boys, or the way that intelligence is presented through Piggy and dismissed by the others. Analysis might consider the way that good and evil are being represented through the setting of the island and the boys' careless, although accidental, damage of the island. The different attitudes are present in the adjectives associated with each boy, or their actions, for example, Ralph's metaphoric 'machine-gunning'.

Pages 6–7

Quick Test

1. Ralph and Simon build shelters for the boys to sleep in, protected from the storms of the island.
2. Simon cares for the littluns more than the other boys do. They look up to him, and he finds them fruit to eat.
3. Roger throws stones from a distance, although he remembers enough of adult disapproval to avoid hitting them.
4. Jack becomes more savage and animalistic. He camouflages himself, losing his sense of self and identity as he becomes obsessed with hunting. When the fire goes out, he doesn't accept responsibility; instead, he is violent to hide his shame and embarrassment.
5. Jack's hunters let it go out while they're hunting a pig. A ship passes by but there's no smoke to attract its attention.

Exam Practice

Answers might include the increasing obsession of Jack in contrast to the practical, protective natures of Ralph and Simon in their different ways. Analysis might include the peaceful natural symbolism associated with Simon, Ralph's exclamative of frustration at Jack's lack of understanding or the semantic field of power and anger.

Pages 8–9

Quick Test

1. To tell the boys that they need to do what he tells them and to make sure they know who's in charge.
2. That it's a monster coming from the sea or the forest. Jack says there's no beast – he's explored. Piggy scientifically reasons there's no beast. Simon says they are the Beast.

3. Killed in an aerial battle, the parachutist lands and is caught in the trees, seeming to move in the wind – and is mistaken for the Beast.
4. They see the parachutist, believe he's the Beast and tell the assembly that they've seen a real monster – Ralph believes them because they're some of the older boys.
5. The boys, led by Jack, still treat it as a game, finding a place for a fort without any thought about the practicalities.

Exam Practice

Answers might consider the different ideas that the boys have about the Beast, and the way their responses reflect their character so far. Analysis might include Golding's use of the third person narrator to explore the list of Ralph's thoughts, suggesting his impatience and loss of control, the **triadic structure** in the darkness and the monstrous imagery or the blunt short sentences showing Ralph's courage.

Pages 10–11

Quick Test

1. They're both trying to get the boys' admiration for their hunting ability but refuse to see it in each other.
2. First, they re-enact the hunt in a tribal manner. After successfully hunting, they mount a pig's head on a stick as a sacrifice to the Beast.
3. He calls a vote to become chief instead of Ralph, but humiliatingly nobody votes for him. He leaves embarrassed and upset.
4. The pig's head, speaking to Simon. It's also the name for the devil, symbolising the evil in the boys.
5. He has a hallucination, because of the heat, dehydration, the fear of the head and his tendency to faint.

Exam Practice

Answers might consider the difference in Ralph and Jack's responses including Ralph's focus on his dirt compared with Jack's use of masks and camouflage. Analysis might also include Jack's increasingly savage attitudes as well as his comment after the mock-hunt about using a littlun and the short sentences as he leaves, showing he is upset. He also uses a language of games and play, showing his naivety. Conflict is also present in the violent **imperatives** of the tribal chanting.

Pages 12–13

Quick Test

1. Crawls out of the forest, finds the parachutist and untangles his body so he drifts away. Then goes to find the boys.
2. The chaotic, frenzied dance – they're angry, frightened and whipped up into a bloodlust. The storm above makes the scene more confusing with thunder and lightning adding to the chaotic, angry **atmosphere**.
3. It gets 'dressed' in light, as though in worship, and washed out to sea as nature claims his body.
4. Ralph accepts responsibility but can't believe what he's done. Piggy tries to find reasons and rationalise it. Sam and Eric pretend they left early.
5. Piggy's glasses – a symbol of intelligence and hope to Ralph's boys as they are needed to start the fire.

Exam Practice

Answers might consider Simon's murder or the fight. Analysis might include the way Golding creates a chaotic, fast-paced and frenzied atmosphere through the list of angry, animalistic verbs. It might also include the ways Golding ironically presents the boys as one unit acting together or the contrasting calm when Simon's body is left on the shore to emphasise the violence of what went before.

Pages 14–15

Quick Test

1. By persuading Ralph, Sam and Eric to confront Jack about his glasses, then leading them to the mountain despite not being able to see.
2. Roger levering the rock so it rolls down the mountain.
3. The officer on the beach intervenes as the boys catch up to him.
4. The officer represents rescue for the boys, and the return of society and order.
5. He decides not to step forward and claim responsibility for leading the boys.

Exam Practice

Answers might consider Piggy's increasing bravery and the ironic timing of his death, or the way that Ralph and Jack come to their final conflict. Analysis might include the rhetoric of Piggy's speech-making or the descriptive language and zoomorphism of the sea at the moment of Piggy's death.

Pages 16–17

Quick Test

1. Moving time or place, setting the mood of the chapter.
2. Frequently ends with a cliffhanger or dramatic climaxes including deaths, fights and separation.
3. Repeating similar events but developing them in some way, for example, Roger throwing rocks to foreshadow Piggy's death or the similarities between the deaths of Simon and Piggy.

Exam Practice

Answers might explore the openings and endings of chapters, and echoed events. Analysis might include ... the semantic field of pressure and heat, and the pathetic fallacy of tension and fear or the pauses describing the officer, suggestive of the lack of understanding from society.

Pages 18–19

Quick Test

1. It's a religious allusion to the perfection of the Garden of Eden.
2. Through the destruction of the boys, as corruption of mankind and the oppressive monstrous way nature is described.
3. At first they're excited and thrilled but they become oppressed by its difficulties.

Exam Practice

Answers might include the contrasting ways the island is described and the increasing oppression of nature around them. Analysis might explore the semantic field of destruction contrasted with the peaceful vocabulary of the island or the representation of nature as a monster.

Pages 20–21

Quick Test

1. Working with boys, Golding saw how they were sometimes bullies, even cruel, and explored what would happen if social restraints were to be removed.
2. He believed in original sin and the concept of evil.
3. Through his accent/grammar and that he lived with his aunt instead of his parents.

Exam Practice

Answers might explore the way that Golding saw bullying behaviour on a smaller scale and how he witnessed groups of children being cruel to one another, even in normal social conditions. On the island, without social control, these differences and cruelties escalate.

Pages 22–23

Quick Test

1. The struggle between what's right and what's justified, as well as the idea that democracy is fragile.
2. Jack's patriotic belief in English superiority becomes jingoistic – he doesn't think about the morality of his actions, but focusses instead on exerting control and doing things his way.
3. The evacuation of the boys as a result of nuclear fears, and the pilot's message about an atom bomb.

Exam Practice

Answers might explore the way that the conch is a symbol of democracy and its fragility reflects the way that Europe's democracy was systematically threatened during the mid-twentieth century through war. Answers might also analyse the misunderstandings of Jack as to what there is to be proud of in British values or that Ralph attempts to keep democracy alive while Jack is happy to ignore it the more power he has.

Pages 24–25

Quick Test

1. *The Coral Island, Swallows and Amazons* and *Treasure Island*.
2. In the other novels there are enemies to fight – pirates and savages – but the boys in *Lord of the Flies* are their own enemies.
3. By reminding readers of the unrealistic, rose-tinted view these books have both of children and of the past.

Exam Practice

Answers might include the contrast in tone/mood from optimistic and naive, to Golding's interpretation. Analysis might consider the colloquial slang and references made by the officer, and the descriptions of a diminutive Ralph.

Pages 26–27

Quick Test

1. He plays around, seeing the conch as an instrument and play-shoots Piggy. He thinks his father will rescue them.
2. He has something in his manner (a calmness) the boys respond to, more than Piggy's intelligence or Jack's arrogant leadership.
3. He recognises the importance of thinking and applying thought in action. He understands the motivations of other people, even if he doesn't know how to change their behaviour.
4. He begins to forget about the signal fire, which suggests that everyone is vulnerable to a lack of civilisation.

Exam Practice

Answers might explore the way Ralph develops his leadership qualities or loses his innocence. Analysis might include the symbolic adjectives of devilish/angelic connotations, the pause in Ralph's speech as he attempts to work out his own behaviour or the increasingly dirty triadic structure demonstrating his physical (symbolically moral and emotional) deterioration and a reminder of his young age.

Pages 28–29

Quick Test

1. Leadership through control, fear and bullying – and how dangerous this is to others.
2. He uses mud as camouflage to create a mask, symbolising his loss of identity and transformation into a savage.
3. He always hates Piggy, abusing him to gain influence with the other boys. He is initially friendly with Ralph but gradually creates divisions in the group to humiliate him.

Answers

4. Sometimes Jack is remarkably childlike – when he's humiliated after challenging Ralph and when he's described at the end. This could be intended to provoke sympathy.

Exam Practice

Answers might explore the way that Jack exerts his control across the novel. Analysis might also include the ways that Jack changes in his opinion of what leadership is or the symbolism of his physical appearance that changes as he takes on a more tribal leadership role. Also, consider the lack of genuine responsibility implied in his inability to accept their reality.

Pages 30–31
Quick Test
1. He avoids him at first, then tolerates him, then comes to value his intelligence and opinion above all others.
2. His glasses (intelligence, science and civilisation) and the conch (democracy).
3. Jack dislikes him for 'stealing' Ralph's friendship, for being inferior to Jack and for his quiet confidence with the conch.
4. Roger pushes the rock that hits him, throwing him off the cliff.

Exam Practice

Answers might include Piggy's insistence on logic and rational thought, or his constant references to science and technology. Analysis might consider the rhetorical questions in persuading the other boys to behave maturely, the confidence in grown-up thinking or the **parallelism** of his question comparing civilisation and savagery.

Pages 32–33
Quick Test
1. The choir, but he becomes more friendly with Ralph.
2. By building shelters and helping the littluns find fruit.
3. He sees its truth, that they should be afraid of the evil in the boys. He sees the parachutist for what it is.
4. Killed (beaten to death) by the other boys in a ritual frenzy.

Exam Practice

Answers might include Simon's association with church-like spaces or his reflective nature, his connection with nature or his role as prophet seeing the truth about the Beast and mankind's evil. Analysis might consider the light imagery suggestive of candles and nature, or the juxtaposition of heroic and sick to describe man or Simon's Christ-like relationship with the children.

Pages 34–35
Quick Test
1. Shy and furtive, a 'dark boy' who keeps to himself.
2. He becomes Jack's second in command and assumes authority on his own for the violence needed to intimidate the other boys.
3. He throws rocks at Henry, foreshadowing the rock that kills Piggy. He 'rapes' the pig and mounts its head on a stick. He sharpens a stick for Ralph's head.

4. Contextually, Roger represents **sadists**, people who take pleasure in hurting or humiliating others, especially when they're able to do so legitimately, such as in wartime and acting against their enemies.

Exam Practice

Answers might include Roger's violent actions or his increasingly violent nature. Analysis could consider the stammering of the twins with the pauses to show their fear of him or the semantic field of violence associated with language of pleasure, for example, 'delirious abandonment'.

Pages 36–37
Quick Test
1. Nightmares and creepers in the forest; the parachutist; the pig's head on a stick; Simon; the boys themselves.
2. Makes him lose hope after he sees the parachutist. He feels the Beast as evil in the boys but can't articulate it.
3. He leaves a sacrificial offering, showing his tribal regression, and then (after Simon's death) tells them it can't be killed, partly to clear his conscience.

Exam Practice

Answers might include the different forms the Beast takes and the different realisations the boys have about its true nature. Analysis could consider the change from the childish 'beastie' to 'beast', the pauses when discussing it, suggesting their inability to articulate their fears and understanding and the rhetorical questions of the pig's head, as well as its almost jubilant **triadic structure**, as though mocking Simon.

Pages 38–39
Quick Test
1. They are 'cheerful' but 'like dogs', suggesting their loyalty.
2. They change allegiances regularly, beginning with Jack then supporting Ralph, then Jack again.
3. It becomes 'Samneric', one name representing their loss of individuality.
4. They are tortured by Jack and Roger, and betray Ralph so that the hunters can track him down – Ralph only escapes because the officer arrives.

Exam Practice

Answers might consider the physical and behavioural similarities, and the way that this leads to a lack of individuality, making them an 'everyman' character. Analysis might include the repeated plural **pronoun**, the adjectives describing their physical appearance or the change in their names to one name.

Pages 40–41
Quick Test
1. Percival Wemyss Madison, the boy with the birthmark, Henry and Johnny.
2. That they're all one group, viewed together, which means they lose their individual identities, especially when compared with the older boys.
3. They have nightmares and talk about beasties. The death of the first boy also haunts Ralph.
4. In Chapter 5, Percival chants his name and address as an 'incantation' to get him home safely. By the end of the novel, he's been so traumatised he's forgotten both.
5. It is assumed he dies in the first fire the boys set, in Chapter 2.

Exam Practice

Answers might consider the littluns fear, the way that they are used to highlight the different attitudes of the older boys or the association of the littluns with vulnerability and death. Analysis could include the short sentences describing the fear of the littluns, the pathos of Percival's crying or the use of anonymous pronouns or plurals to refer to them rather than as individuals.

Quick Test

1. Dictatorship (one person in control) and democracy (everyone has a right to be heard).
2. Democratic.
3. Dictator.
4. The conch symbolises democracy, including its fragility. The final fire symbolises the destructive power of dictatorship.

Exam Practice

Answers could explore the different boys associated with each type of leadership and the changing power balance through the novel, the power struggle between Ralph and Jack as symbolic of the wider context of the novel and particular fights/tension between the two. Analysis might include the triadic structure of leadership qualities (all three needed for the ideal leader), the exclamatives showing Jack's excitement over punishment and dictatorship or the connection of physical power with animalistic language (chattered, ape) rather than intellect.

Pages 44–45

Quick Test

1. Through his clothing changing and increasing dirt.
2. Increasing violence, savagery and tribal behaviour.
3. Scientific knowledge and understanding, and the democratic rules of the conch.
4. The return of the adult world, and therefore, civilisation, to the island.

Exam Practice

Answers might explore the ways the different boys see civilisation and the lack of it or the gradual changes in the removal of social rules and morality. Analysis could include pauses in Ralph's language showing his lack of understanding, the noun 'toy' to suggest the playfulness and lack of seriousness with which society is sometimes taken, the language of dirt in Ralph's description or the symbolism of the officer's uniform, for example, the naval elements and the purity of 'white'.

Pages 46–47

Quick Test

1. The boy with the birthmark (accidental fire), the parachutist (adult world), Simon (the boys, in ritual frenzy), Piggy (Roger's rock).
2. Pretend or play-acting (Ralph's machine-gunning, the hunting) or the boys' inability to act violently (Jack's hunting, Roger throwing stones).
3. He's affected by it; he participates in killing Simon and attacks Jack.

Exam Practice

Answers could include the deterioration of the boys' violence, from play fighting and self-restraint to murder. Analysis might consider the violent verbs associated with the boys, the **syndetic structure** suggestive of continuous aggression.

Pages 48–49

Quick Test

1. Bravado and action – claiming he'll hunt the Beast even though it doesn't exist. Later, violence and control.
2. It distorts people's behaviour and stops them thinking logically.
3. Themselves, or fear itself.

Exam Practice

Answers could include the different responses the boys have or the way that fear makes them react at different times, for example, the hunting, the storm/Simon's death, Jack and Ralph's final conflict. Analysis could consider the pauses showing Piggy's difficulty in speaking of what he's afraid of, Ralph's matter-of-fact tone and negative language associated with fear.

Pages 50–51

Quick Test

1. Beelzebub, a name for Satan. In the novel, this is represented by the pig's head and Simon's hallucination.
2. The belief that mankind is born innately evil.
3. Worshipping of idols – both himself as chief in the way the boys treat him and of the Beast by leaving it a sacrifice to appease it.
4. The church-like settings he goes to, feeding the littluns, and his martyrdom while telling the boys about the true nature of the Beast.

Exam Practice

Answers could explore the way original sin is represented through the boys' deterioration into violence, the conflicting representations of the island as the Garden of Eden or Hell or the religious imagery associated with Simon and Jack. Analysis might include the allegorical references to snakes (signifying Satan), the imagery of idolatry and sacrifice associated with Jack and the description of Simon's change once he has realised the innate evil of mankind.

Pages 52–53

Quick Test

1. His loss of belief that his father will rescue them, his changing dreams and loss of memory about the fire.
2. They become more violent and corrupt the island paradise.
3. He represents the adult world where war and destruction still rage.

Exam Practice

Answers might consider the changes in Ralph or the other boys, the destruction of the island from paradise to hell, the divisions and conflict between the boys or the increasingly deliberate violence. Analysis could include Ralph's childish language and assumption of a traditional family, Piggy's matter-of-fact description of adults or the contrasting language of the final lines.

Pages 54–55

Quick Test

1. Merridew (grown-up, authoritative but civilised), Jack (child, equal to the others), Chief (tribal, savage leader).
2. Removing clothing especially the uniform that marks them as a social group, although Ralph keeps some of his. The savages wear mud as war paint.
3. Losing the memory of why the signal fire matters and the language to express its importance is losing the identity connecting him with home.

Exam Practice

Answers might include the way the boys separate into different communities, from choir to hunters, the way they swap uniforms for war paint or the way boys lose their memories of home. Analysis might include the sense of awe and fear that different identities inspire or the symbolic use of paint and clothing.

Pages 56–57

Quick Test

1. His jealousy over Ralph's friendship with Piggy, their disagreement over the importance of the fire versus hunting and that Ralph has been voted leader.
2. Ralph tolerates Piggy, but is sometimes dismissive – he seems to accept him rather than genuinely like him.
3. He realises Piggy's intelligence and loyalty. Ralph increasingly respects Piggy's ability to think logically.

Answers

Exam Practice

Answers could include the changing relationships and the way that one friendship declines as another becomes closer. Analysis might consider the semantic field of power and barriers or the language associated with happiness/joy.

Pages 62–63

Quick Test

1. AO1 – focussed, structured answer to the character in question; AO2 – how Golding uses language, structure and form to convey his ideas; AO3 – links to social, historical and literary context; AO4 – accurate spelling, punctuation and grammar.
2. 45 minutes to write, including around five minutes to plan.
3. To gather ideas and put them into an organised, coherent structure. (AO1)

Exam Practice

Ideas might include the following: Jack's change from near-adult to child to chief, shown by his name; the changes in friendship with Ralph; he creates a division between the boys so he can lead instead; his changing identity through his appearance; his increasing obsession with hunting, violence and control; by the end, all the officer sees is another anonymous child.

Pages 66–67 and 72–73

Use the mark scheme below provided to self-assess your strengths and weaknesses. Work up from the bottom, putting a tick by things you have fully accomplished, a ½ by skills that are in place but need securing and underlining areas that need particular development. The estimated grade boundaries are included so you can assess your progress towards your target grade.

Pages 68–69

Quick Test

1. AO1 – focussed, structured answer to the character in question; AO2 – how Golding uses language, structure and form to convey his ideas; AO3 – links to social, historical and literary context; AO4 – accurate spelling, punctuation and grammar.
2. 45 minutes to write, including around five minutes to plan.
3. To gather ideas and put them into an organised, coherent structure. (AO1)

Exam Practice

Ideas might include the following: Jack's near-grown-up state at the beginning of the novel; the contrast between biguns and littluns; the responsibilities of different boys and their different maturities (Piggy/Ralph/Simon contrasted with Roger/Jack); the role of adults – the war, the parachutist mistaken for the Beast, the officer and their symbolic meaning about the innate violence of the adult world.

Grade	AO1 (12 marks)	AO2 (12 marks)	AO3 (6 marks)	AO4 (4 marks)
6–7+	A convincing, well-structured essay that answers the question fully. Quotations and references are well-chosen and integrated into sentences. The response covers the whole novel.	Analysis of the full range of Golding's methods. Thorough exploration of the effects of these methods. Accurate range of subject terminology.	Exploration is linked to specific aspects of the novel's contexts to show a detailed understanding.	Consistent high level of accuracy. Vocabulary and sentences are used to make ideas clear and precise.
4–5	A clear essay that always focusses on the exam question. Quotations and references support ideas effectively. The response refers to different points in the novel.	Explanation of Golding's different methods. Clear understanding of the effects of these methods. Accurate use of subject terminology.	References to relevant aspects of context show a clear understanding.	Good level of accuracy. Vocabulary and sentences help to keep ideas clear.
2–3	The essay has some good ideas that are mostly relevant.	Some quotations and references are used to support the ideas. Identification of some different methods used by Golding to convey meaning. Some subject terminology.	Some awareness of how ideas in the novel link to its context.	Reasonable level of accuracy. Errors do not get in the way of the essay making sense.